THE WORLD AND THORINN

THE WORLD AND THORINN

by Damon Knight

Published by Berkley Publishing Corporation
Distributed by G. P. Putnam's Sons, New York

for KATIE, at last,
and for our son JONATHAN

Contents

1   How Thorinn Goryatson learned he was not the son of his father, and descended into the Underworld without wishing to do so.   1

2   How Thorinn lost his sword in a lake, and became a stonemason to get it back.   13

3   How Thorinn discovered that it is easier to fall into paradise than to get out again.   26

4   How Thorinn roasted two fat waterfowl for his supper, and what happened thereafter.   40

5   How Thorinn entered a treasure cave and found a magic box that could speak, albeit foolishly.   48

6   How Thorinn fell five hundred leagues in a day and a night.   67

7   How Thorinn was the guest of demons, and how he repaid their hospitality.   77

8   How Thorinn was made captive by a flying engine that carried him deeper into the Underworld.   95

9   How Thorinn tried to cross a river, and found it unlike other rivers.   107

10   How Thorinn entered a town of seven towers, and dissolved its enchantment by accident.   118

11   How Thorinn tried to fly without success, and built a bladder instead.   131

12   How Thorinn battled flying engines in their cavern, and solved a riddle wrongly.   146

13   How Thorinn died and was brought to life again, but resented it.   154

14   How Thorinn was offered dominion over the world at a price, and learned his true name.   167

1

How Thorinn Goryatson learned he was not the son of his father, and descended into the Underworld without wishing to do so.

In the days of King Alf there was a house in windy Hovenskar at the hub of the world, where the sky turns round the Pipe of Snorri. The house was of sods, with a stone roof, for no other sort of roof can stand against the winds that blow, this way and that way, over cold Hovenskar as the sky turns.

Now Hovenskar is like a yellow bowl, and from this side of it to that side is three days' journey. Long is the spoon with which the gods eat porridge from that bowl! Northward can be seen the half of Snorri's Pipe, a gray-green column three leagues in thickness, yet so tall that it seems to prick the sky like a needle; and around it the sky swings, half light and half dark. Therefore at high noon there is an eye of darkness peering over the rim of Hovenskar, and at midnight an eye of brightness. And the wind blows from the dark to the light, this way and that way over Hovenskar.

In this unlucky place, in the days of King Alf, lived a man called Goryat and his three sons, who were outlaws driven out of Kjelsland. Goryat and the two elder sons were gray-skinned Low-

landers, four ells tall, with tusks like daggers; but the youngest son was pink as a Highlandman, and stood no taller than Goryat's belt-buckle. Though he had a withered leg, he was sturdy and quick, and could jump higher than his own head. Thus he was called Thorinn, which is a kind of flea.

Now it happened on the last day of King Alf (when a roof-tile dashed his brains out) that for thousands of leagues, even unto the land of the Skryllings, the earth became flat where it had formerly risen, and arose where it had been flat. Rivers left their banks, lakes became marshes, the air was one black scream of birds, and everywhere cook-pots rolled out of kitchens, while the cooking-wenches tumbled after.

But of all this the four of Hovenskar knew nothing. They knew only that Snorri's Pipe had begun to roar, with a sound that thrummed in the bones and could not be shut out, though they stopped their ears with their fingers; that their bodies had turned light, as in a dream; that there was an earth-shock that made men and horses dance on the ground like lice on a griddle; and that bits of the sky were falling like frostflakes.

Before they could gather their wits about them, one of the horses, a mare with foal, had broken her leg in the peat bog, and the rest were scattering up the high curve of the valley, from whence it was half a day's work to drive them home again.

Now this was a weighty matter, and it grew weightier still on the second day, when the other four mares went dry. Goryat took the finest of the remaining horses, a stallion of two summers, and sacrificed him to Snorri. But the demon did not leave off roaring: instead, as Goryat finished his prayers, there was a second earth-shock, and from the well nearby came the crack of stone breaking, and all the water ran away into the Underworld, leaving the well dry as a skull.

Then the two elder sons urged their father to leave Hovenskar and fare southward, but the old man, whose hand was still heavy though his mane had turned white as frost, would have none of it. "In all the Midworld there is no safety for me or those of my blood save in Hovenskar," said Goryat to his sons. "Nor may Thorinn leave, for I have sworn by Wit and Bal to keep him." Thus did the two sons learn from their father's lips for the first time, though in truth it was plain to be seen, that Thorinn was no blood brother of theirs.

"But if we sacrifice another horse, we may go empty-bellied through the winter," said Withinga, the eldest son.

"Moreover, it's plain enough that Snorri wants no horses." Thus spoke Untha, the second son. "Is he the demon of waters, or not? When the horse was offered, he was vexed and broke our well."

"We must give him something better," said Withinga.

"Idle is boasting when the hands are empty," Goryat answered. "What, must we fare to Skryllingsland and bring back a sacrifice?"

"Not so far as that," Withinga said. And he pointed his chin toward the hillside, where Thorinn was leading the horses to the spring.

Goryat said then, "Would you make me an oath-breaker? I tell you, I swore to keep the boy until Snorri takes him."

Untha rose, and pointed to the black mouth of the well. "Then give him to Snorri."

So it was agreed. When Thorinn came down, suspecting nothing, they said to him, "Go into the well, see whether it can be mended." Then when he was in the well, they pulled up the bucket and covered the well-mouth with a great stone, and prayed over it.

The Flea lay upon his back, hands behind his head, the knee of his good leg cocked over the other. His left leg was shorter than the right and had always been so; he could grip a horse with his thighs well enough, but when he was afoot, the bad leg was too feeble to bear his weight for more than a moment, and so he hopped everywhere (though Goryat's sons always said the short leg was good for walking on the hillside, so long as he took care to go withershins).

The blades of yellow grass formed a wall close around him, shielding his body from the wind that rustled overhead. Through half-shut eyes he could see the wavering patch of brightness that was the sky. Drowsy scents of grass and blossoms were in his nostrils, mingled with the faint but pungent smell of horse that clung to his leather garments. He could hear the stiff grass-blades crackling as insects crawled among them; the snort and stamp of the horses farther up the hillside; and, more distantly, the unending drone of Snorri's Pipe.

Deliciously hidden and at ease, more than half asleep, he was

daydreaming of distant mountains and brightly-dressed people
when a new sound roused him.

He started up on one elbow, listened: there it came again. He
pivoted with one hand on the matted grasses, sprang up. Far
below, over the thousand moving waves of yellow grass, he could
see Goryat's steading in the bright half of the valley—the house
with its roof of gray stone and its thread of smoke bent by the
wind, the horse-barn, the meathouse, the tanyard, the well, all
tiny as pebbles. Near the house a mannikin stood; its mane was
only a dot of yellow. The arms were lifted; it shook a fist. After a
second the hail came again: . . . *ooorriii.* . . .

Thorinn waved his arms in answer. The tiny figure gestured
with one hand, then turned away. It was already loping slowly toward the house when the sound arrived: . . . *ooom doww.* . . .

They had thought of some other task for him; that was only to
be expected.

Breathing the keen wind, Thorinn forgot all disappointment as
he raised his head. It was mid-morning, and where the tip of the
Pipe touched the sky beyond the valley rim, the dome was split by
a clean arc that soared high over Thorinn's head, dividing the sky
into pale light and greenish darkness. Half the valley below was
daylit; the other half lay still in deep night, pricked here and there
by the witchfires of fallen sky-stuff. Over in the peat bog, wisps of
night mist were rising like ghosts; dew still sparkled in the grass
along the daylight edge.

As the day wore on, the arc in the sky would creep around the
rim of the valley. One could almost see it move; Thorinn had lain
many an hour on the windswept hill, watching it, until he fell fast
asleep, and the horses roamed where they would.

Tits and fieldfares were busy in the cropped grass around the
spring, quarreling and chirruping over the bits of grain they found
in the horse droppings. Hawks were awheel over the high rim; but
in the dark side, Thorinn knew, owls and nightjars were stirring.
Northward from Hovenskar, it was said, there were night creatures that never ventured into daylight, but followed the darkness
eternally, around and around. Someday Thorinn would go and
hunt them; Goryat would give him leave when he was a man. The
world was good, though Snorri rumbled.

Above him near the outcrop and the spring, the eleven giant
horses turned their heads alertly. Thorinn filled his lungs and

shouted. "Ho, Biter! Ho, Stonehead!" The horses snorted, tossed
their manes; Stonehead, the old stallion, showed his wicked teeth.
Thorinn bent his knee, leaped over the grasstops, alighted two ells
higher on the slope, leaped again. The horses, pretending fright,
wheeled and lumbered away. Thorinn's leg pumped furiously; he
bounded, leaped like a grasshopper after the soaring horses. He
passed two stragglers, nervous young colts. The earth trembled,
bouncing him higher. Blood burned in his veins; the wind whipped
his cheeks, made his eyes smart with tears. Head down, his massive hindquarters bunching like fists, old Stonehead flew before.
Stones and clots of turf spattered Thorinn like hail. He was flying,
lungs afire. Into—the yellow—sea—and out. Ahead, the stallion's
round eye glinted; the old horse turned, laboring upslope. In two
breaths Thorinn was beside him; a final leap, and the rough mane
was against his face, his arms and thighs gripping the shaggy neck,
while the world wheeled.

Winded and utterly happy, Thorinn clung to the stallion's neck.
After a plunge or two, earth and sky steadied around him; obedient to his will, the old stallion, who could have flung him five ells
if he chose, stood snorting and trembling. Thorinn reached up,
grasped a thick hairy ear at the root, pulled gently. The stallion
dipped his huge head, turned and sprang.

The other horses, standing at gaze a few hundred ells away, fell
upward into distance. The steep yellow bowl of the valley came
plunging up, the wind whined in his ears—down, with a bone-
breaking jolt, another leap—down, another. Bounding below, the
tiny shapes of the houses grew larger with each dizzy arc. The
stallion's neck strained against Thorinn's cheek; they were flying
like the wind, they would leap and never come down!

The descent grew shallow, the hillside was behind them; now
they were bounding across the level earth toward the stone-roofed
house, and the gray figure beside it. Thorinn recognized Withinga,
tall as the house-eaves, in his stained leather jerkin and his belt
studded with metal bosses.

Obedient to Thorinn's touch, Stonehead planted his hooves, slid
to a bone-jarring halt. While Withinga watched sourly, Thorinn
vaulted to the ground, slapped the old stallion's rump. Stonehead
snorted, wheeled and bounded away toward the distant shapes of
the other horses high on the hill.

"Do you want to break your neck, Flea?" Withinga asked, taking a stride forward.

"When Snorri calls, man must answer," said Thorinn. He hopped back, expecting a blow, but Withinga only stared at him for a moment, then said: "So it is. Come, the Old Man has a task for you."

Thorinn followed him around the moss-grown sods of the house. Under the weight of the roof, the sod walls had bulged year by year until the house had lost all its squareness and was shaped like a cheese. Beyond in the dooryard, Untha and old Goryat squatted at the well-curb, beside the empty leather horse trough. They looked up as Withinga and Thorinn approached; Untha, who had been scratching the bare earth idly with his dagger, gaped witlessly, showing tusks as long as Thorinn's thumb. His yellow eyes, slitted like a goat's, stared at Thorinn as if he were a stranger.

Without speaking, Withinga sank down beside the other two. Squatting in a row, the three stared at Thorinn. Their massive, yellow-maned heads were on a level with his. Beyond them, the split sky arched over the rim of Hovenskar. At last Goryat spoke. "The well is broken."

"Did you call me down here to tell me that?" asked Thorinn in honest surprise.

"Hold your tongue and listen," said Goryat. "It is in my mind that the well may be mended. Therefore, jump into it and see."

Thorinn hopped to the well-curb and looked down. The deep shaft receded into darkness, past the leather thong and the dim round shape of the bucket; he could not see the bottom.

"How shall we mend it?" he asked.

"With stones," grunted Withinga. "The fool asks, wise men must answer. Go down, Flea."

Thorinn bent toward the dark receding shaft, from which a faint cool breath arose; then a new thought struck him. "If this should be long in the doing," he said, "who will cook the dinner?"

The two brothers glanced at each other again, and Withinga stroked his chin with a taloned gray hand. "Well asked," he said grudgingly. "Also, who will fetch peat for the fire, and tend the horses?"

"And milk the mares, supposing they turn fresh again, and

make cheese?" put in Untha, scowling and toying with his dagger. "That is no work for a man."

Thorinn stared from one to another, for their words made little sense; but Goryat said, "Peace," and gave them a hard look under his frosty brows. "Witlings have I for sons. The thing is decided." In his hands was a little framework of yellowed ivory carved with runes, a magical implement which Thorinn had seen only twice before. "Go down."

Thorinn hesitated, but he felt a pressure as if an invisible hand had been laid along his back, and he realized that the old man had put a spell on him, a geas: go down he must. He bent and picked up the bucket thong. He tugged at the end of it, where it was knotted around one of the stones of the curb, found it secure, and backed over the rim of the well-mouth, lowering himself hand under hand. The three white-and-yellow-maned heads turned to watch him. They disappeared over the rim of the well, but a moment later, as he descended, they came back into view, peering down. The three silhouetted figures seemed to rise and become foreshortened, the horizon sank, the ground bulged upward like water closing over his head. Clods and an occasional pebble, scraped loose by his feet, rebounded below. After a moment or two he heard something strike the bottom. Cold air breathed up past him. The edge of the leather bucket touched his thighs. Holding the thong with one hand, he pulled the bucket up free of his legs, hung a moment, and dropped.

The bottom drifted nearer. Dimly he saw it, bent his knees, took the shock. But the bottom of the well was tipped beyond his expectation, and it threw him against the side, making his head ring.

He straightened himself and breathed deep. How cold it was down here! and no wonder, for the water they got from the well, before it went dry, had been cold as ice. That was natural, for the deeper you went, the farther from the warmth-giving sky. Thus it was colder here on the floor of the ancient ocean than it was in the Highlands; colder again at the bottom of the well; and if you could dig deeper still into the earth, eventually you would come to the land of eternal ice, the Underworld, where Snorri ruled.

Go down.

Thorinn crouched and felt for the source of the steady slow current that breathed up around his legs. Oddly, although the air was cool, it seemed warmer than the earth and stones around him. His hands found an opening, half choked with mud. So far as he could tell, the rock table under the well had broken, and he was now crouching on a tilted slab of it that had fallen and stuck.

He heard a sound, twisted to look up. The mouth of the well was a disk of brightness, surrounded by concentric half-circles of gray reflected light. The sound was repeated, and Thorinn saw a tiny black dot rise to the well-mouth, bob and disappear.

For a moment he could not believe it; then he stood hastily and shouted, "Hi! Don't pull up the bucket! How am I to get up again?"

A maned head appeared, in silhouette against the sky, and looked down at him silently. It vanished; another appeared at a different place; then it, too, was gone. "Ho!" shouted Thorinn, hearing his voice boom up the shaft.

He listened. Over the slow sighing of the wind, a sound so familiar in Hovenskar that it was heard only when it changed, he caught the grumbling voice of Goryat.

"Lift your end!"

Footsteps scraped on the pebbles beside the well-curb. Then something dark came into view and hung suspended in the middle of the disk. The broken circle of brightness around it flickered and vanished, the light on the walls turned gray and went out. A stony clang echoed down. The black air pressed close to Thorinn's eyes, and seemed as heavy to breathe as water. There was a long pause, then another clang.

Thorinn's heart was leaping, but he reached for his wallet calmly enough, found the wooden light-box and uncovered the window of mica at the end. The pale witchfire of the sky-stuff inside brought his arms back in ghostly dimness, and a vague circle of the dirt wall; but though he shielded it with his hand, it would not reach the top of the shaft.

He waited, saying to himself, "It was a joke," but in his belly he knew better. Not for any prank would glum Goryat or his lazy sons have lifted those two great stones, the broken slabs left over from the roofing, which had lain half sunken in the earth beside the house for as long as Thorinn could remember, and laid them one atop another across the mouth of the well.

He listened. Dimly from above, vibrating through the slabs of stone, came the deep rising and falling tones of Goryat's voice.

Though he could not make out the words, the rhythm was familiar. What was it? Then he knew: the invocation to Snorri, the one Goryat had chanted when they had sacrificed the horse.

The men of Hovenskar lived by their horses; for the mares to go dry was a disaster. A prudent man does not offend the gods; therefore Goryat had sacrificed a stallion. When Snorri refused the gift, what more natural than to offer a boy instead?

Fear was a cold knot in his stomach. He took a deep breath, another. The walls of stone around him were like a shirt laced too tight. He felt half smothered already, and yet he knew there was no lack of air. It was thirst that would kill him—that would take days. To die of thirst in a well! Never mind, he had time, a precious gift—three or four days, perhaps, before he grew too weak.

What else? He had his short sword, really an old Yen-metal dagger of Goryat's, in its leather scabbard; the broad leather belt it hung from, which might be useful in climbing; his wallet and its contents, which he now examined—light-box, fire stick and tinder, a few crumbs of cheese, a strip of dried horsemeat, and a few odds and ends, colored pebbles and the like, which he had picked up because they were pretty. Then there were the clothes he wore, shirt and breeks of buckskin, horsehide shoes, and the thongs that wrapped his calves: a rope of sorts might be made of all these things together.

Thorinn sat down on the floor of the well and hugged his knees for warmth. In the glow of the light-box, which he had placed on a stone beside him, he saw a sudden flutter in the air: something small and gray had darted up zigzag to vanish in the darkness.

Thorinn stared upward, mouth open, then snatched the light and raised it over his head.

At first he saw nothing. Then a small gray creature detached itself from the wall, spread a pair of membranous wings, and swooped erratically to the other side. It was a wingmouse, one of the darkness-loving creatures that sometimes flew out of the cave on the valley slope two leagues above. Where had it come from?

He turned the light on the opening at his feet. This was a narrow black gash at the side of the well, no more than a span in width, but he saw now that it widened below.

Kneeling with his forehead pressed against the mud and pebbles, he was able to see a shelf of muddy earth a few ells away. It did not extend all the way under the opening, however, for he could just make out an edge of blackness on the near side—a second, deeper hole. Mud and pebbles cascaded slowly down into the darkness. The current of moist air was feeble but steady against his fingers; it seemed to rise straight toward him.

Thorinn sat up, feeling his heart beat. Who cannot take the short way home must take the long, as the saying was. If he could somehow reach the cave of the wingmice. . . .

Go down, agreed the voice in his head. He pulled out his sword, jabbed the point into the lip of earth over the opening. A wedge of dirt and stones came away and drifted down into the darkness; he listened, but did not hear it strike. He pried loose another wedge, and another. When he had made the opening large enough to admit his body, he paused and again looked in. This time, in the dim glow of the light-box, he could see a tumbled mass of muddy earth and stone, sloping like a funnel.

After a moment's thought, Thorinn unwrapped the thong from one leg of his breeks and tied it securely around the light-box. Kneeling again over the hole, he carefully lowered the box and let it drop. In darkness now except for the glow that came up through the hole in the well-bottom, he stood and listened. Goryat's voice still rumbled overhead. He stared upward a moment silently in the darkness, then turned and lowered himself feet first into the hole.

The dim-lit cavern rose around him. He landed, staggered, caught his balance. Crouching, for there was little head-room here, he picked up the light-box and brushed away the clods and gravel that had fallen on it. He held his breath to listen. The silence was so deep that he could hear the thud of his own heart.

The low dirt ceiling, porous and stained reddish-brown in places, formed an irregular dome. Ceiling, walls and floor were mud-splashed; stones bigger than his head lay as if tossed about. The mound of mud and stones sloped away channeled and rutted. In one direction it disappeared under a great tilted stone, leaving an opening no more than a span high; in the other it went almost level into the darkness.

Thorinn untied the thong from his light-box and wrapped it around his calf again. A faint current of air blew in his face as he moved down the slope.

Just over his head, tongues of some crusty reddish material hung from the ceiling. Thorinn tugged at one curiously, and found that it was metal, rusted so thin that it broke in his hand. Below,

the runneled mound grew shallower and seemed to end in a level
floor, with a few scattered boulders. As he descended, the ceiling
rose, forming an arch overhead, as if he were in the bore of some
giant earthworm. The patches of rusty metal grew larger and
closer together; he recognized others, twisted and broken, among
the heaped earth and stones at his feet. Farther away, the arched
roof of the tunnel glinted silvery through the rust. Thorinn moved
along one wall, examining it as he went, and at last stopped in
wonder: between the dots and patches of rust, wall and ceiling
alike gleamed with silver-gray luster. The tunnel was lined with
Yen-metal, the incorruptible; yet it had rusted away to nothing in
places.

With each long step he took, another yellow segment of the tunnel bloomed out of the darkness; presently it seemed to him that
he was not moving at all, but the tunnel was leaping toward him.
The tunnel was like a yellow eye with a vast black pupil at its center, and Thorinn began to feel a terror of it because it was so huge
and so close. When he turned, he saw another yellow eye behind.
After each step the silence pressed in on his head like a sound too
loud to hear.

He stopped when he was tired, gnawed a bit of his horsemeat
and lay down to sleep. When he awoke, the yellow eyes of the
tunnel were staring at him as before. He gnawed the strip of horse-
meat again, but that only increased his thirst. He put two small
pebbles in his mouth and sucked at them as he went, and that
helped a little.

Now the tunnel began to change; there were slight irregularities
in the even curve of the ceiling and walls: yellow glassy knobs, in
shape like candlewax, but hard as stone. As he went on, these irregularities made the tunnel even more unpleasant; they were like
blinking eyelashes around the great staring eye.

He had lost all account of the distance he had traveled; he
knew that it must be ten leagues or more, and yet he could not escape the sense that he was only leaping up and down, while the
stone danced toward him.

He smelled the water before he heard it, a distant rushing sound
in the tunnel ahead. Moment by moment it came nearer, and the
breeze freshened: now he saw that the tunnel floor was broken by
a great hole, ten ells across, that went down out of sight in undu-
lating level stripes of brown and cream-colored stone. Great

blocks of rubble were heaped on either side of it, and above them he could make out a black cavity vanishing into the ceiling. It would be no great matter, he thought, to leap from the boulders into the shaft above, and it was narrow enough to climb without a rope: but he would need both hands free. He unwrapped the thong from one leg and used it to tie the light-box to his forearm.

He climbed the blocks and turned the light-box downward; he could not see the bottom, but the sound of the water dinned in his ears. As he gathered himself to leap, something curious happened: he took a step he had not intended. Beneath him, the water roared.

He struggled in terror, but the stones dropped away and he was falling. *Go down,* said the voice in his head.

2

How Thorinn lost his sword in a lake, and became a stone-mason to get it back.

It was the distant, thunderous roaring of the water that brought him up out of darkness. He was sprawled on wet stone, retching feebly. His legs were still in the water, which lapped at his middle rhythmically and insistently, over and over in the same place. When he tried to crawl out of its reach, he found his legs too heavy to move. He belched up a watery surge of vomit against the stone. After a while, groaning, he managed to drag himself an ell or so away from the water, and rolled onto his back.

The light-box was still bound to his arm, but its glow was so feeble that he could barely see it. When he looked up, the darkness pressed close against his eyes. The sound of the water roared endlessly, off in the darkness. He could remember the water plunging up over his head, the helpless motion, the falling. . . .

There had been an unaccustomed freedom when he rolled over on the stone; something was missing. He felt for the scabbard at his belt; it was there, but it was limp; the sword was gone.

After an interval, some faint sound in the darkness brought him struggling up on one elbow. He listened, but the sound was not repeated: he heard only the steady, tumultuous roaring of the water.

On his right cheekbone there was a thumb-sized lump, still welling blood, and his shoulder felt as if someone had clubbed it.

A touch told him that the light-box was ruined. One end was split, the mica missing and all the sky-stuff washed out of the compartment except for a few shreds clinging to the soaked wood. The dim glow came from these.

The knots in the wet thong were too much for his fingers, and at last he attacked them with his teeth, jerking at them stubbornly until they loosened enough to slip the light-box free. Holding it with care in both hands, he pried the wooden cap off the other end. The mica there was still whole.

He unlatched the lid, raised it, and probed delicately in the second compartment. It was half full of chill water, in which he could feel the sodden sky-stuff afloat.

Thorinn let out the breath he had been holding. He fumbled over the stone with his free hand until he found a hollow place, then tilted the box over it, pressing the sky-stuff against the inside of the compartment and straining the water out between his fingers.

He remembered that he must put aside a portion of the dark sky-stuff. He unfastened his wallet and tipped the water out of it, then pinched up a good lump of sky-stuff between thumb and finger, and laid it carefully at the bottom of the wallet.

Now, if there was enough of the bright sky-stuff left. . . . Thorinn scraped the inside of the ruined compartment with his forefinger, brought it up with the fingernail dimly glowing, and touched it to the sodden mass in the other half of the box. The sky-stuff bloomed into pale light, dim but beautiful to his eyes.

He shut the lid carefully upon it, then aimed the mica end of the box this way and that around him. He was sitting on a smooth flat rock that sloped gently to the water, and ran away featureless into the darkness on every other side.

Now that he had light, his first care was to recover the few strands of sky-stuff that had escaped between his fingers when he poured the water out. He dipped them up out of the puddle one by one, dried them as best he could by shaking them gently, and deposited them in the box again.

Next he thought of his hurts. Dark sky-stuff, moistened and bound to a wound, was said to be healing; but he had none to spare, nor any other simples. As for magic, he knew none; he could cast runes, and find lost objects sometimes, but that was all.

He climbed stiffly erect. His sopping garments clung to him, his shoes squelched when he took a step; even his hair dripped cold down the back of his neck. He turned toward the distant roaring sound and slowly began to hop along the edge of the water, holding the light-box before him.

After ten steps a black wall of rock gleamed out of the darkness. It went nearly to the water and rose overhead farther than his little light would reach. He turned away from the water, up the slope. After a few steps the stone on which he had been walking ended and gave way to other slabs, more uneven, higher and of a smaller size, while the wall curved gradually back, away from the roaring sound, until it ran parallel with the water.

In thirty paces more, Thorinn came to a head-high shelf on which some leathery fans of fungus grew. He pulled them down, found them white and doughy inside, with a strong stale odor. He nibbled at one, found it palatable, then ate all the rest and looked for more. But he found no others of that size, only a mass of larger ones joined together in long rows, dead and as hard as spearwood.

He turned away in disappointment, but after a moment, thinking better of it, went back and broke loose some of the dead fungus. It came away in a long staff, like a loaf of bread. He examined the inner surface closely in the glow of the light-box: it was porous and tinder-dry. Insects had tunneled through it, leaving portions of the mass so eaten away that they collapsed under his thumb.

Thorinn knelt on the cold stone, opened his wallet and got out his fire stick. The tinder was a sodden mass of fiber. Thorinn untied it and spread it out on the stone: it might dry enough to be of use, he supposed, but that would take days.

He dried his hands as well as he could by rubbing them along the rock, then picked up the staff of fungus again and began to break off small pieces. But his touch dampened them in spite of all he could do, and at last he broke the staff into two parts and began rubbing the ends together to grind off chunks and fragments. When he had a pile of these, he laid the rest of the fungus aside and picked up his fire stick. It was wet, but the plunger still slid freely enough in the cylinder. Thorinn took it apart, shook a few drops of moisture out of it, then, holding it braced against the stone between his legs, sat patiently driving the plunger in, over and over, until the cylinder grew warm to the touch and the inside was dry.

He opened the fire stick then, wedged the cylinder upright into a crack in the stone, and used the shreds of fungus to pick up other shreds, preserving their dryness, and drop them into the fire stick. He put the plunger in, drove it down smartly, removed it: the shreds of fungus were glowing bright orange. He tipped them out carefully into a pile of the finest fragments and dust of the fungus; they glowed for a moment more, then went out.

On the third try, the little fire caught. Thorinn protected it with his cupped hands, blew gently on it, fed it sparingly with tiny splinters, then with bigger ones, and at last had whole chunks and staves of fungus blazing.

The yellow light danced high, reflecting glints from the rock wall for a distance of five or six ells, before it vanished into shadow. Peering up between his hands, Thorinn thought he could make out a vague glimmer that might be the ceiling.

He crouched to the fire, soaking up the warmth with hands and face, then stripped off his soaked clothing and stood near the flames, turning himself like meat on a spit until at length he was dry and warm. The blood that welled slowly from the wounds in his cheek and shoulder began to clot.

Feeling stronger, Thorinn walked along the wall of rock collecting more staves of fungus, which he piled near the fire; then he turned his shirt and breeks inside out and sat down to dry them. He emptied his wallet, putting the lump of sky-moss carefully aside in a cranny of the rock, and examining the rest of his belongings for the first time to make sure they were safe. He laid his possessions out carefully on the rock, and propped the wallet open to dry along with his shoes.

The leather of his shirt steamed, turned a lighter brown. He pulled it right side out again and put it on, then the breeks. They were not thoroughly dry, but they were warm inside, and would do. He chose a long, heavy staff of fungus, laid one end of it in the heart of the fire. His shoes were as wet as ever, but he put them on, gathered his possessions into the wallet and hung it from his belt.

By this time the end of the fungus staff was blazing; he lifted it out of the fire. Yellow flames continued to curl around its tip, and when he held it overhead, shading his eyes, it cast a ruddy light that made the cavern visible for a dozen ells or more on every side.

The rock wall rose in one receding shelf after another back into the shadows. Tipping his head back now, Thorinn could make out the broken rock surface of the cavern ceiling. But although he walked down to the edge of the water and held the torch high, he could not see the other side—only the dark, glassy, faintly moving surface of the water and the dim slope of the bottom under it, shelving down into darkness.

He turned away from the roaring sound and followed the edge of the water in the other direction. The rock wall curved closer, became broken and covered with gray nodules of fungus; the stone shelf underfoot narrowed until there was barely room to walk, then gave way to heaped boulders. The thunderous roaring receded behind him, but another water-sound rose ahead. Holding his light out over the water, he saw the gleam of a swift current.

Now the ceiling began to dip lower. Thorinn was picking his way from one water-rounded boulder to another at the foot of the sheer face of rock. The ceiling curved down, the shelf broadened out again into two flat stones . . . and between them the water ran in a curved dark torrent, brilliant as glass, into a narrow slot of darkness under the wall.

On the other side of the outlet the shelf broadened again, and behind it was a tumbled mass of boulders. Thorinn leaped, landed safely.

As well as he could judge, the cavern at this end was some twenty or thirty ells broad, and the ceiling might be as much as thirty ells high in the center. On this side, the ceiling slanted sharply down to the talus slope of boulders at the base of which he stood. Fungi grew here and there on the stones. Thorinn picked all the smaller ones he saw, ate some and put the rest into his wallet. He found another long staff of dead fungus and tore it down for a spare torch.

The roaring grew louder as he circled the lake. Out across the dark water, an orange spark leaped into view: it was his fire, on the other side. He watched it for what seemed a long time, until it abruptly winked out again, and he realized he had passed the wall of rock that jutted out to the water.

His torch was burning low. He paused to light the second one, and in its brighter flare, something white and vast rose out of the darkness. The roaring filled the cavern now as he moved closer; it stuffed his ears with noise. He shouted and could not hear himself. The air was full of flying droplets, drifting in faery arcs, winking and vanishing. The white water dropped thunderously into the lake and burst into white mounds of spray. Thorinn could dimly make out the shapes of rocks like giants' skulls behind the curtain of water. He could not see the top of it, and his torch was smoking and dimming now as he tried to move nearer; the wet air was putting it out. Thorinn retreated until the torch burned brightly again, then began to climb the heaped boulders, working his way toward the waterfall.

The air was less damp at this height, and he was able to approach within twenty ells or so of the cataract. He was halfway up the cavern wall now; the boulders would take him no higher. He raised the torch. The dim light glimmered back from a hole in the rocky ceiling, from which the torrent sprang out greenish-white and curved into space.

One look confirmed what he already knew: he could never get back up the way he had come down.

As he sat on a boulder, his eye was caught by a tiny glimmer of brightness under the dark water, far off toward the middle of the lake. He stared at it under his hand, and in a moment was almost sure that it was his lost sword: but it might as well have been at a thousand leagues' distance for all the good it was to him.

Weariness took him as he sat, and he began to think how good it would be to lie and rest, near the fire for comfort, though indeed, except for his wet shoes and breeks, he was comfortable enough. The air in this cavern was cool and fresh; there was no wind. . . . Here he began confusedly to imagine that the cavern had the ceaseless wind of Hovenskar blowing through it, and that the gray-maned horses were lifting their heads beyond Goryat's stone-roofed house, which somehow was all mingled with the wall of the cavern, and the smoke as it rose from the smokehole leaning crooked in the air. . . .

He came to himself with a start, to realize that he had all but dropped the smoldering torch. The torch was half out, a black stub crawling with fire-worms, and the thin, acrid smoke drifted aslant.

Thorinn's head rose to follow it. Since the air was fresh, there must be some way for it to come and go. The two holes that he knew of were both filled by the moving water.

Stung to wakefulness, he rose and began to climb, following the motion of the air and the dim path of the smoke from his torch. In a few minutes, questing along the top of the heap of boulders, he found a crevice in the wall into which a faint current of air was moving. But the crevice was no bigger than his fist.

At the lower end of the cavern, where great slabs of the ceiling had fallen and lay heaped all anyhow, the thin smoke of his torch eddied and drifted. Stooping to peer between two slabs, Thorinn felt cool air breathing on him. He held the torch nearer, singeing his hair in his excitement.

Behind the rock slabs, an irregular passage ran away into the earth; it was two ells high at the opening, and seemed to grow larger as it went. Thorinn put one arm in, tried to follow it with his head, but could not.

He drew back and examined the boulders. The smaller of the two was half buried by a clutter of other stones; the larger lay almost free on the slope, supported at its lower end by another slab. Thorinn got his fingers around the edge of the large stone, braced himself and pulled, without effect. He tried again, nearer the top, but it was no use; the stone weighed as much as a horse.

He rested, feeling weak from hunger and exertion. If he only had a lever, a pole, anything, to pry the larger slab up and out, away from its support at the bottom!

A picture came into his head, but he pushed it aside. Never mind: where there was one such passage there must be others. He blackened the stone with the stub of his old torch to mark it, and went on. He leaped the gap at the lake's outlet, circled back to his starting point.

His fire was gray ash and embers. He built it up again, then began to climb the terraces that sloped away behind. The rock wall here was full of promising oval hollows, but every one turned out to be no more than a niche in the rock. He made the whole circuit of the cavern once more before he was sure: there was no other exit from the cavern.

Into his mind came the image of the sword, dim yellow under the water. If he could only get it back, that would be his lever. But it was impossible.

He prowled aimlessly around the heap of boulders awhile, then went down to the water's edge and stared out over the black surface.

Even to find the sword in the water was out of the question. If he could fly in the air, then the thing would be easier. He saw the lake as if spread out below him, with the sword gleaming in its depths; and on the shore he put two white stones for markers, pointing the direction. Well, there were no white stones, and even if there were, they could not be seen in the dim light of his torch.

Then he saw how it could be done. After a moment he turned and walked toward the cataract, gathering dead fungus as he went. When the white mountains of spray showed in the light of his torch, he turned aside and began to climb.

At the place where the sword gleamed up at him from the bottom of the lake, he made a fire on the flat top of a boulder. He climbed up the slope a few ells, and made another fire; then he climbed again to verify that the two fires, one behind another, pointed toward the sword.

He climbed down the slope and stood looking at the lake. The water was as shallow here as on the other side, but it shelved away rapidly until within a few ells the light of his torch could no longer reach the bottom.

Thorinn took off his shoes and breeks, then his belt and wallet, and laid them on a stone. The air was cool on his bare skin. He hopped into the water, wincing. The stone was slippery. Crouching to support himself with one hand, he moved forward another step and was ankle-deep; another, calf-deep; another, cautiously, and his leg went in to the knee.

He staggered back, trying to turn; his bad foot went out from under him and the cold water choked off his yell.

Smothered, gasping, he floundered up to shore again. He had tried to hold the torch above water as he fell, but the splash had put it out. He was wet all over, as wet as he had been before.

Some while later, hugging his misery, he sat staring out over the dark water. The sword lay on the bottom, not more than fifteen ells from where he sat. But the lake was too deep for wading; he could not swim; there was no boat, or anything to build one. If only the lake were solid rock. . . .

Thorinn sat up. In his mind he saw a level road of stones under the water, straight to where the sword lay. His heart bounded; he turned, scanning the slope in the dim firelight for stones of a proper size. There were plenty of them, slabs level on top and bottom, about half an ell in thickness.

The first three went easily enough; he laid them in a straight line out into the water. The fourth was harder to carry; the fifth, though it was no bigger than the others, he could not even lift higher than his shanks. He staggered out with it nevertheless, dropped it in place, lurched back to shore.

He rested, built up his two fires above on the slope, and went back to work. As the causeway lengthened, instead of one stone he must put down two, one atop the other, to bring the topmost to the surface. His first stones he had laid a handspan apart, but since he had begun to pile them one on another, each column must lean against the one before it, lest it fall. Even so, more than once the second stone slid off the first.

Then the bottom grew deeper still, and three stones in each column were needed. Three times he tried to build a column of three stones, and three times it collapsed. Thorinn splashed back to the shore cursing, and flung himself down on the cold stone trembling with weariness. But he got up again, and laid two stones side by side for a foundation, then one above, and a fourth stone on that. In this way he built another column, and another.

Time passed. The fires burnt low and he built them up again. Looking down from the height, he could see his stone path straggling out into the water, less than halfway toward its goal.

He lay down again to rest, dropped into exhausted sleep, and woke from dreams of eyeless goblins to find himself cold and in the dark. His fires had gone out. He collected fungus to build them again, drank a little water from the lake, eased himself behind a boulder.

The columns now must be four stones tall: two stones, then two more above, then one, then one more. When he had built one such column of six stones, his arms were like lead, his breath burning his chest. It was impossible to go on. He lay cursing himself feebly, then got up and began another column.

Now time had stopped, and there was only the pain of his

labor. He counted the columns and there were nineteen. The twentieth must be five stones high: he built it in courses of three stones, then two, then two, then one, and one. So with the next, and the next. Each time he climbed the slope for more stones, he could look down at the causeway and judge whether it was holding to the right direction or not. He slept and ate again.

The twenty-sixth column was six courses tall—four stones, then three, three, two, two, and one: fifteen stones, to advance his causeway the width of one stone. After another dazed interval, he counted the columns again, and there were twenty-nine.

Thorinn pulled his torch out of a crevice, waded back out across the tops of the columns. He held the torch trembling over his head, peered down. There it was, deep down, straight ahead, glimmering golden under the water.

He went back, wedged the torch into its crevice again, climbed the slope for more stones. He built his last column carefully—four stones, then four more, then three, three, three, two and two. The final course came above the surface of the water. He went back for a torch, wedged it in between the two topmost stones.

The sword gleamed up at him out of darkness, looking near enough to touch. He could see the wooden handle carved for a close grip, the dull place where the tang went into the handguard, the bright double edge. It lay on the smooth rock bottom among a few pebbles, waiting.

Thorinn tied one end of his thong around one of the topmost stones, the other around his waist. His hands were like wood. He climbed gingerly down and around the last column, groping for footholds. The cold water stung his wounds. The water surged, lifted at his body, trying to upend and drown him. He clung to the end of the causeway, pressed his cheek hard against the stone. What remained was such a little thing—to climb down another ell or so, take the sword, climb up again into the air.

Thorinn filled his lungs, squeezed his eyes shut, lowered himself into the water. Water was in his eyes, his ears, blinding and deafening; the water lifted him, swung him helplessly while he struggled for his life. His hands found the thong; he pulled, came up choking and gasping.

The trouble was, perhaps, that he had tried to climb down the wall of stones as if it were in air; but the unfamiliar lift of the water had tricked him, thrown him off balance. Caution, then, was

his enemy. He must plunge boldly into the water, let himself sink
to the bottom, take the sword, and pull himself back to safety.

It was harder to do it than to think of it. Twice he tried to
throw himself off, twice his muscles refused him. At last he
climbed down until the water was up to his chest, then closed his
eyes as before and lunged forward.

At once he found himself choked, floundering, turning. He
could neither sink nor rise. He pulled himself out again, coughing,
spewing up water.

He sat on his causeway and looked back at the length of it,
dimly shining under water in the torchlight. What bitterness to be
defeated after such labors! But without the art of swimming, he
could not move under water; the treacherous stuff would not even
let him sink.

A thought came to him, and he stood up wearily, looking down
at the stones of the causeway. He bent, seized one of them half
under water and hoisted it out, groaning with effort. The wet stone
weighed nearly as much as he did, and in his weakness he could
barely hold it. Surely, if he threw himself into the water again, carrying such a stone in his arms, he must sink.

He gave himself no time to consider. As he climbed awkwardly
around the last column, he slipped, felt himself falling. The water
plunged past him. The stone was dragging him down; water was in
his eyes, nose, ears. . . . He felt a blow against his knuckles,
knew he was on the bottom. His grip loosened and his body
floated backward, but he seized the stone again. His lungs were
bursting. He forced his eyes open, saw a stinging blur, a
gleam. . . . Holding the stone with one hand, he reached out desperately, felt his fingers close around wood and metal.

Somehow he found the thong with his other hand, pulled, rose.
He burst into air—he was alive. The sword, the sword— His heavy
arm came up, and in his hand, streaming water, was the bright
metal.

Levered upward, the slab trembled, moved a finger's breadth,
then began to slide. Thorinn pulled the sword out of the way,
leaped back. Turning majestically, the slab rumbled down the
slope in a dancing cloud of smaller stones. It struck a boulder
halfway down, tilted, came to rest. Stones pattered, fell silent. A
haze of dust particles hung in the air.

Thorinn examined his sword anxiously, but the hard Yen-metal had taken no hurt. The point was as sharp and straight as ever; the double edge was not even nicked.

Cool air breathed past him into the exposed passageway. In the light of the torch, it was curved, lusterless, smooth-walled, unequal in its cross section—tapering almost to a point at ceiling and floor. It sloped gently upward out of sight.

Thorinn turned for one last look out into the darkness of the cavern. He had slept, rested, eaten all he could hold of the young fungus he had gathered. The rest—there was little enough—was in his wallet.

He discarded the torch, which was too smoky to be used in a small space; for convenience, he strapped the light-box to his arm as he had done before. He entered the passage and gingerly began to work his way down it in the yellow glow. For the first twenty ells or so it was not bad; then the passage narrowed so sharply that he had to crawl, dragging his wallet behind. The passage turned and twisted like a serpent, this way and that, now left, now right. With each upward turn Thorinn waited for the voice to speak in his head, but it did not, and his spirits rose; but at last the passage took a definite downward slope and widened again.

Thorinn crawled out into a black echoing space—another cavern, much smaller than the last. The opposite wall gleamed in the light, streaked and knobbed with some glassy substance that seemed to have melted like tallow and hardened again on the stone. But when he touched it, it was the stone itself.

A trickle of water came from somewhere above and dripped from the bottommost knob with a melancholy sound. Thorinn cupped his palm under it and drank a sip, but it was bitter.

At the far end of the cavern he found two level passageways, one opposite the other, as if they were parts of a single tunnel that happened to intersect the cavern. Thorinn took the left-hand branch. Almost at once the passage widened, the ceiling rose and became a dome three ells high. In the middle of the passage lay something enormous, circular and dark.

Thorinn stared at it suspiciously. It made no move; neither did it have any eyes or limbs, so far as he could see. It had the chill hardness of iron; it was wrought metal, the largest piece he had ever seen—like a giant's shield, ten spans across, having a circular hole pierced in it of three spans' width. This hole was not in the center of the shield but to one side; through it he could see the brown, scuffed floor of the passage.

He knelt and laid his palm curiously on the metal near the rim of the hole: and the massive shield turned under his hand as if it were afloat.

Thorinn sprang back, hand to his sword. But the shield was slowly rotating upon some hidden pivot, returning to its former place. When the hole was where it had been before, it stopped.

A second time Thorinn bent forward, put his hand on the shield and felt it turn. When he took his hand away, it swung slowly back to rest. What could be the use of such a thing, here under the earth, unless it was some springe or man-trap?

As he hesitated, a sound came to his ears—the faintest of whispering or rustling noises; it seemed to come from beneath the shield. The sound died away, then returned: a sound like that of some small creature crawling, scraping along in the space under the shield . . . no, not like that, but like some sound that he knew. Then he had it: wind in the grasses.

The thing was impossible, yet the more he listened, the more certain he became. Using the tip of his scabbard, he prodded the shield. Under the circular hole, brown rock moved past, then a sudden glint of brightness. The wind sound grew louder; a warm breath of air arose. The bright lozenge expanded to a cramped circle, then filled the hole in the shield.

Thorinn's breath had stopped. He was looking down into depths of silver light and brown-green shadow. There were stripes of darker brown, diminishing in a curiously painful way; at last he realized that they were tree-trunks, gnarled and huge, that dropped darkening through space until they were tiny as needles' ends at the bottom.

He could not doubt his senses. Somehow he had got above the Midworld, for there it lay below him.

Go down, said the voice in his mind.

3

How Thorinn discovered that it is easier to fall into paradise than to get out again.

In the spring, when the pleasure pods were ripe, everybody in Pink Circle went on a picnic into the wildgreen along the river Wend. Grasshopper men went, two by two, arms linked as they soared through the air; dough women with their fancymen went, panting and wallowing; the gray-bearded Knowers went, hobbling, leaning together, and sat on the grass to watch the young people.

First the unsexed little girls and boys would collect food from the foodvines that grew in the wildgreen, spicy orapples and sweet nanaberries, meatlets in clusters, hamsaniges from the hamsanige bushes. Meanwhile the young men and women would be gathering cushions from the cushionleaf trees and arranging them in circles on the cool sloping lawns, near enough to hear the pleasant gurgle of the Wend. The song-girls would tune up their vine-strung rebecks and there would be singing, then the food gathered by the unsexed little boys and girls would be heaped up and eaten; then there would be jumping and running contests, games for the children, jokes and argument for the elders; and finally, one by one, the people would wander off into the wildgreen until each had

*found a ripe pleasure pod gaping invitingly, with its soft water-
melon-pink lining like a doughgirl's youknow. Each one would
search until he found a pleasure pod that just fitted, long thin ones
for the grasshopper men, round fat ones for the dough women,
short stunted ones for the children and fancymen. The pleasure
pods for the dough women had to be almost on the ground, for
the dough women were clumsy and could not jump; but the fancymen could scramble up the tall curled vines, and the grasshopper men could jump, twist as they jumped, and land gently on
their backs inside the pleasure pods. The pods would dip a little
lower with the weight of the people, hanging down from their long
strong flexible vines, and the lip of each pod would slowly close
until the pod was shut tight, with the happy person inside like a
worm in a flossweed. What dreams they had then, what pleasures,
twitching and moaning with their pleasures so that the hanging
pods trembled, first one, then another, then a whole row at once!*

*When the skylight dwindled and the shadows turned greener in
the wildgreen, the pods would open and the people would climb
out, their limbs soft, their faces shining with remembered joy, eyes
soft and faraway, their movements slow. But some of the pods
remained shut as the people wandered back toward Pink Circle;
there were some who liked the pleasure pods so much that they
would not come out for a day, or two days, or a week or a week-
week sometimes; and in fact, every spring when the pleasure pods
ripened, there were always some dark old pods from the year before that hung, heavy and shriveled, on the dead vines, until the
wind, or a boy climbing, or a heavy bird alighting knocked them
down and they rolled into the carpetvines. These were old people
mostly, who had nothing to gain by coming out of the pleasure
pods, but there were young ones too, some every year, and even a
child occasionally, who stayed in the pods and never came out.*

*What more can be said of Pink Circle, that longgone place,
than that it was perfect, an elysium, without discord or bad food?
Thus it was, thus it had always been, until that black day unfore-
told by Knowers, when a nonperson climbed down into the wildgreen. Yes, he came from the sky, for a doughgirl saw him: he
opened the door like a yawn in the sky, and fell, and caught himself in the trees of the wildgreen; and thus he came into the world
of men.*

Go down, said the voice; but the puzzle was how to do it. The revolving shield was a kind of door, yet there were no stairs below, not even a pole to climb. It was a door for birds, not men.

Bracing himself against the slow impalpable pressure that was trying to force him down, he put his head through the hole and saw that the nearest tree ended in a crown of tangled stalks, some green, most brown and dead, against the sky two ells away. The glare of the skylight, so close to his face, dazzled him and made dark spots float before his eyes.

He drew back, perplexed. It would be no great matter to lower himself by his hands through the hole, then swing and let go, to land in the treetop. But unless he could somehow prop the shield open, it would be moving while he hung from it, and might catch him by the fingers.

Go down.

Thorinn took off his belt and leg-thongs and tied them together as he had done before, with the sword dangling at the end. Holding the shield open, he dropped the sword and swung it in a slow arc, farther each time, until it caught in the treetop. The first time it was only lightly tangled, and came free again; the second time it held fast. When he tugged on it, a branch of the treetop nodded toward him. He knotted the other end of the cord to his wrist, then doubled his legs and swung them down through the hole.

The sky above his head was one bright dazzle. The cord tied to his wrist led nowhere; he no longer knew which way the tree was. What if the sword had come loose from the branch? The shield was turning, it would close on his fingers. . . . He let go, reached for the cord as he felt himself afloat, falling. He pulled the cord in, hand over hand; at last it tightened, and now he could see the tree like a great green hill tilting, leaning toward him. Twigs lashed him, then the tree struck like a giant club and he was clinging somehow to a branch, safe, dizzy, breathless, and triumphant, in the warm wind.

The skylight was screened by leaves above him, turning the world into a shimmer of silver and green. All the leaves were in faint constant motion; the tree itself swayed slightly, rocking Thorinn back and forth as he clung to the branch. Faint and dizzy, he clambered into a more secure position atop the branch, then worked his way down along it until he could brace his back against the trunk.

Some bright insect, of a kind Thorinn had never seen before, drifted by, hovered for a moment, and was gone. He saw now that there were golden fruits among the leaves. A trickle of sweat ran down his ribs. Indeed, it was warm here, and no wonder, so close under the sky.

The thong ran away slanting, disappeared among the bright leaves overhead. He tugged at it, saw a responding movement above. He untied the thong from his wrist, wrapped it loosely around a branch, and began to climb. He found the sword snugged up against a fork in the branch, and freed it. He tugged at the thong, and after a moment it came up. He buckled the sword-belt around his waist, put the thongs away in his wallet.

He had hoped to get a better view of the countryside from here, but the dazzle was so great that he could see nothing. His leather shirt was stuck to his back; sweat stung his eyes. He began climbing down the branch.

Farther down, where the limbs were bigger and closer together, he was able to drop from one to another. The glare lessened rapidly, but he felt as warm as ever; he was stifling in his leather garments. He stopped where a broad limb made a convenient perch, peeled off his shirt, and felt better at once. A breeze fingered his bare chest and back. How good it felt, and what a fragrance there was in the air!

The shirt was too bulky to go into his wallet; he tied the sleeves together and hung it around his neck. Then his legs began to feel all the stiffer and hotter because his body was so cool and free, and he took the breeks off too and tied them around his waist.

As he descended again, he began to catch glimpses of the ground through the branches. It was carpeted with vines and grass, only less green than the leaves around him. Now he began to realize how incredibly tall the tree was. He dropped from one branch to another, then the next, and still the ground receded below him.

As he paused for breath, he heard a distant shrilling of voices below. He crouched, listening. There they came again, nearer. Two piping notes, poot-toot, then a chorus that echoed them. Then a deeper voice, boom, boom, boom; then the high voices again. He could not make out the words.

From where he stood, he could see a little patch of greensward between the branches. As he watched, a flash of color crossed a corner of this patch and was gone. He was not sure what he had seen—something flame-colored and moving, and an impression of a face tilted toward him.

Startlingly near, a voice called in two clear notes. Boom, came the answer, not far off; then there was a rustling in the branches below.

Thorinn flattened himself against the trunk. The flash of color came again, and stopped. Down there on the grass, something round and bright was looking up at him. He could not make it out; it was more like a flower than a man, but it had eyes and a face. It made no threatening gesture, but simply stood and gazed up at him. He saw its mouth open; the lips were red. Poot-toot!

The leaves of a nearby branch threshed violently. Turning, Thorinn saw something gray and agile clasping the branch, swinging itself up, coming upright. Another thrashing sound, and another, and another. The things were all around him, and now there were more of the bright-colored ones below, all standing and gazing up, while the gray things, booming, sprang toward him among the branches. They were men or demons, gray-skinned like Goryat and his sons but impossibly thin, with arms, legs, and torsos like twigs. Boom, boom, from one side and the other, echoing among the leaves; and from below, poot-toot, twitter.

Thorinn stood with his back against the tree, sword in hand, trying to see all ways at once. But the gray things, in a half-circle around him, came no nearer. Hairless and naked, they had no weapons; they smiled and gestured, showing their empty hands.

Cautiously Thorinn put his sword away; this set off another volley of boomings around him, twitterings below. The branches swayed again; now other agile bodies came swarming up the tree. These were children, half the size of the gray men, some pink-skinned and to all appearance human, some twiglike and gray. All of them were chattering, piping, booming at once, those in the tree and those below.

Thorinn swung himself down to the next branch, then the next. The children and the twigmen followed him, keeping their distance; below, as the branches thinned, the bright ones drew back.

He inspected them from the lowest branch: they were not half flower and half human, as he had thought. The bright, soft parts of them were garments that might have been made from gigantic flower petals, veined, crumpled at the edges, saturated with color.

Under these, their bodies were round and plump, and, indeed, he now realized, they must be women. Among them were a few gray and shriveled creatures whom he had hardly noticed before; they were clad like the women, and had bright eyes and wrinkled faces. They all stood in a polite semicircle, waiting for him to descend.

Now that he knew they meant him no harm, Thorinn began to feel a new embarrassment. He had never been with strangers before—Goryat and his sons were all he had ever known. How would they expect him to behave?

When he dropped to the ground, another clamor went up; the circle moved inward, while all around him twigmen and children were dropping like overripe fruit. Thorinn was surrounded by smiling pink faces, bright petal-garments of scarlet, deep blue, yellow. When one of the women caught sight of his leg and his wounds, her face changed at once and she began making sounds of distress. In a moment the women were all around him, gently touching his withered leg, his cheek and shoulder, staring up into his face with such dismayed expressions that he could not help laughing. Anxious cries ran back and forth through the crowd; then they were all moving, carrying Thorinn with them.

The bright alien faces bobbed around him, the trees turned skylight into a rich green gloom, the grass was seductively soft underfoot and the slope led him irresistibly downward, so that everything that happened seemed to have become curiously ordinary. They passed through an explosion of bushes, waist high, with thick soft masses of white flowers. From the trees hung green and golden fruits, gourds, seed-pods like twisted ribbons. Fallen trees were everywhere, with vines growing over them.

The bushes thinned to isolated clumps, the trees drew back, and now he was at the edge of a clear place, a slope of bright green grass that curved gently down to the marshy bank of a river. Beyond the silver water another green bank arose, another stand of trees; beyond them were mountains that met the sky. The air from the river was cool and fresh; on the near bank, scattered in little groups, the people were sitting, lying; children squatting, leaping up, running. Someone threw a ball of bright orange into the air; a twigman leaped after it, straight up, higher, incredibly rising; he caught it in his mouth and dropped back, to shouts of applause.

Thorinn would willingly have joined them in spite of his shyness, but the crowd urged him to the right, along the edge of

the forest. After a few ells the shrubbery drew back into a little
bay, in which giant vines hung looping and twisting from a tree,
higher than Thorinn's head; from these vines depended soft green
pods or shells, curved and fat, two ells long. Some swung lightly
and were open to show a tender pink interior, while others were
shut tight and hung heavy to the ground. The people urged him
toward one of the empty pods, and showed him by gestures that
they wanted him to lie down in it.

While he stood hesitating, one of the closed pods stirred, split,
began to open. A glint of pink showed within. A plump woman
emerged, rosy-faced, with dreaming eyes. She was like someone
just awakened from a long sweet sleep. With languorous movements she stepped out, picked up her petal garments discarded on
the grass, slowly put them on. A faint smile curved her lips. She
wandered away across the greensward; behind her, the pod
swayed empty.

Not liking the look of this, Thorinn backed away. The women
caught at his arms, touched the wounds on his face and shoulder,
pointed again to the empty pod. It was as if they were trying to
say that the pod would heal him.

Thorinn tried to explain with gestures that he had medicine of
his own. But they were slow to understand, and at length he had
to get a pinch of sky-stuff out of his wallet and point repeatedly to
it, then to his wounds.

This set off a flurry of excited conversation, with much waving
of arms and movement back and forth. The people brought forward one of the oldsters, who squinted wisely at Thorinn, stroked
his straggly beard, and piped a few words of gibberish. At this, the
whole flock of them set off again, down the slope this time, drawing Thorinn along. They led him into a circle of people gathered
around a heap of fruits on the grass. Some of the people got up to
make room while others sat down, and when the confusion ended
Thorinn found himself seated with a plump woman on either side.

A child scrambled into the circle, plucked a pale greenish ovoid
from the heap and handed it to one of the women, who offered it
to Thorinn. He took it dubiously; it was cool in his hands and had
a strange fragrance, but he was hungry, and bit into it boldly. It
was soft and pungent, the flavor sweet and acid at the same time;
the cool juice ran down his chin. The exposed meat was a startling
emerald green. Thorinn instinctively spat out what was in his

mouth. He was thinking better of it and about to take a second bite, when one of the women took the fruit away from him gently and offered him another sort. This was flattish and pale brown, with a texture almost like bread; inside was something firmer. Thorinn bit through the soft outer layer into a salty, fibrous substance. It was a deep pink in color and tasted almost like cooked flesh of an unfamiliar sort; yet the thing was a fruit, for it had a stem and the remnants of a husk.

The people watched him eat, with broad smiles and cries of encouragement. As he was finishing the bread-meat thing, a group of children ran into the circle with curled leaves in their hands. In the leaves was dark sky-stuff which they must have gathered in the forest.

One of the oldsters came forward, inspected the contents of the leaves with great gravity and care, then called for a fruit, which was given to him; it was a smallish, golden-yellow one. He squeezed it in his hand until the clear juice ran into the sky-stuff. He stirred and molded the drenched moss with his knobby fingers, then, apparently satisfied, picked up a mass of the sodden stuff, leaned forward, and began to plaster it carefully over the wound in Thorinn's cheek. After an instinctive start, Thorinn sat still and let him do it. The sticky juice made the sky-stuff cling; it felt agreeably cool on the fevered lips of the wound.

When he was done, the old man called for a leaf, which he smeared with sap from a green stalk; then, carefully pinching the lips of the wound together, he spread the leaf over sky-stuff and wound, and pressed it down firmly. When he had done the same for Thorinn's other wounds, he examined the withered leg and wagged his chin sadly. Then he squatted back on his heels and made a sweeping motion over his head, three times, staring intently into Thorinn's eyes. Thorinn, although he had no idea what was meant, made signs of agreement and gratitude, and the old man went back to the other side of the circle.

Thinking to repay them for their kindness, Thorinn opened his wallet and brought out a few of his treasures, pebbles of various colors, part of a weasel's skull, a bit of crystal. This last he presented to the old man, while the others crowded around twittering with excitement; then he handed out the rest at random, including a scrap of cloth that had been part of a garment of his own until he outgrew it, afterward a rag used by Goryat and his sons to pol-

ish the bosses of their harness; Thorinn had saved a piece because
it had bright figures of birds and people woven into it. The people
took these gifts with every evidence of pleasure. Some of the
women and children offered Thorinn more fruits, each one of a
different sort, and he continued to eat with good appetite.

It was clear that he had somehow got into the Highlands,
though how he had done it was a puzzle; for the trees, though
taller than any he had ever seen, were no more than twenty or
thirty ells in height, yet they touched the sky; and even here, at the
bottom of the slope, the sky seemed close overhead. But these
people in their dress and appearance were nothing at all like the
Highlanders Goryat and his sons had spoken of; nor had Thorinn
ever heard them mention any place of such warmth and brilliance.

The people were all friendly, but not one could understand him
when he spoke, or utter any but their own outlandish noises. He
questioned one after another, saying, "Hovenskar," "Snorri's
Pipe," "the Lowlands," and making gestures, but all he got in return was a new outburst of twittering.

The more he observed them, the more puzzled and uneasy he
grew. There were at least five sorts, the plump wobbling women,
the twigmen, the oldsters, the children of all sizes, and another sort
of men whom he had taken for children at first because of their
small stature; but they were wide-shouldered and well-thewed, and
Thorinn saw them here and there clipping and kissing the women.

Most of the women, the oldsters, and some of the little men
wore petal garments, but the others were as naked as Thorinn
himself now that he had laid aside his sweaty leather shirt and
breeks. They had no weapons of any kind, nor, indeed, any thing
made with hands. They must be persons of quality, if one were to
judge by their soft hands and feet and their merry expressions; yet
there were no servants or bond-slaves among them, so far as
Thorinn could see. They came and went, as aimless as children.
They seemed as curious about Thorinn as he about them, and
there were always some few around him, fingering his skin and
hair, but they all lost interest quickly and went off to join some
game, or wandered into the trees.

When he had eaten his fill, he picked up his bundle of garments,
not liking to leave it behind, and went to ease himself in a patch
of low ground-vines at the edge of the trees, where he had seen
others doing the same. The place had a rank smell, yet not so much

as might have been expected; the broad brownish-green leaves
were curled up and clasped into lumpy bundles here and there,
and when he had accomplished his needs, he saw them crawling
slowly, like crippled snakes, to cover what he had left.

Thorinn watched them for a moment, marveling, then turned
back down the slope. After a few paces he stopped and spread out
his bundle of garments, meaning to use the leg-thongs to tie it together more compactly. At once he was surrounded by children
with alert and curious faces; they squatted to watch him as he
worked, reached out now and then to finger the leather of breeks
or wallet, chattered and piped among themselves. Thorinn did not
hinder them, except to keep them from prying into his wallet; but
one boy, bolder than the rest, plucked up the sword before
Thorinn could stop him and drew it half out of the scabbard.
Alarmed and angered, Thorinn sprang at him, pushed him
roughly, and snatched the sword back.

The boy lay sprawled on the grass, his head half lifted, his
mouth an O. The other children had fallen silent and were staring
at Thorinn. The boy's eyes slowly filled with tears. While the
others made mournful noises and wrung their hands, he got to his
feet. With dragging steps he moved away toward the shrubbery.
Thorinn called after him, but he did not turn. He went to the pod-
vines, stood a moment with hanging head before an empty pod,
then climbed in and lay down inside it. The pod slowly closed
around him.

Thorinn noticed that the other children had backed away, leaving a clear circle around him. Their faces were pale, their eyes big.
A questioning call came up the slope; one of the children answered briefly. Another question, another reply. Other voices
boomed, piped.

Thorinn buckled the sword-belt around his waist, quickly
finished wrapping the shirt, breeks and wallet into a bundle and
tied it with the thongs. Carrying the bundle in one hand, he moved
down toward the river. To either side, up and down the long green
meadow, he could see dots of faces turned to watch him. All the
people seemed to have stopped what they were doing; they were
motionless and silent.

Thorinn kept going, turning now and then to look back; but no
one followed him.

The meadow sloped down into weedy grass and sedge, became

a marsh. Thorinn waded out between heavy clumps of grass, in cool water up to his knees. Little yellow birds burst out of the marsh-grass before him, fluttered erratically for a moment around his head, then dropped out of sight. Up the river, where the stream made a gentle bend, he could see larger birds standing in the water, their long necks looping; they had red breasts and iridescent wing-feathers. Skylight sparkled in the droplets that fell from their beaks.

He stopped where the marsh-grass ended and the muddy bottom grew deeper. To his left, he could see down the river a matter of half a league or so before it disappeared between two gentle hills. To the right, the river curved only a few hundred ells away. Beyond, over the treetops, he could see distant mountains and a faint bright thread that might have been a waterfall. The river ran silver-smooth before him. On the opposite bank was another green slope, narrower and weedier than this one, then trees, then mountains. The sky was bright and blank overhead. He had hoped to see some mark in the sky, but there was none; he would have to wait until nightfall.

He hopped back through the shallow water. Above him on the slope a few of the people were standing watching him; others had gone back to their games, but the little circles around the heaps of food seemed to have broken up. He could see groups of children who seemed to be carrying something toward the shrubbery, passing other groups coming back.

As he approached, he saw that the people were making ready to leave. It was the remains of their meal that the children were carrying. They dropped their armloads in the vines, went back for more. Nearby, he could see a few pods opening, people climbing out. The people were drifting slowly together, all moving in the same direction, forming little moving groups, some with arms linked. Their voices were cheerful. None approached him as he walked up the slope, but a few smiled.

One of the children, a half-grown girl, stood by the pod-vines and waited for him. She gestured toward one of the pods and said something. There was a questioning note in her voice, and she stared earnestly into his eyes.

Thorinn looked at the pod, which still hung heavy to the ground. All the others were open and empty, except one or two, farther back in the tangle, and they looked brown and old. One had fallen from its brittle stalk and lay dark on the ground; the broad-leafed vines had crawled over it, almost hiding it from view.

Thorinn turned to the pod again, thinking of the boy. "Is he still inside?" he asked. She looked at him blankly. He made a pushing motion, then touched his sword, gestured toward the pod. After a moment she seemed to understand. She repeated his gestures, then asked him something else in her piping voice.

Thorinn looked around. The people were drifting away upriver; these two were the last ones left. "Isn't he coming out?" Thorinn asked. He crouched and laid his hands beside his face, closed his eyes as if in sleep. He straightened, pointed to the pod again.

The girl looked puzzled, but repeated his gestures. She came closer, looking into his face, and said something twice over, with great earnestness.

Surely he could make her understand. Thorinn crouched again, imitating the boy asleep in the pod, then mimed coming awake, the pod opening, the boy stepping out.

The girl stared at him. She spoke in a falling cadence; her eyes and mouth were sad. With one hand she made a gesture Thorinn did not understand. They looked at each other for a moment, then the girl turned away to follow the others, who were already distant down the long strip of green.

The pod hung motionless on the vine. Thorinn prodded it with his foot experimentally, moved it a hand's breadth, but there was no answering movement within. He considered whether he should cut the pod open. Did she mean the boy was never going to come out?

Moving listlessly, she was nevertheless slowly catching up to the others. Thorinn hesitated a moment, then decided to leave well alone, and followed her.

Scattered along the grassy bank, the people drifted away before him in twos and threes; the children and twigmen, for the most part, had gone on ahead; the old people, the women, and the women's men strolled behind. Their voices were muted and gentle. In a few paces Thorinn had caught up with the girl; he slowed down to keep pace with her, but although she glanced at him once, she did not speak, and after a moment, losing patience, Thorinn went on ahead.

Where the long green meadow narrowed, the people were filing into an opening in the forest. He could glimpse their bright petals bobbing between the trees. The trail wound gently upward, never steep or difficult, between shrubs with unblemished bright leaves, flowers, vines, trees with hanging clusters of fruit; here and there it curved to avoid a fallen tree. The ground was softly carpeted everywhere. The bushes had no thorns.

Thorinn slipped past the ambling women and old people where he could do so without rudeness on the narrow trail, and eventually had passed all but the twigmen and children, who were now out of sight. The trail was still plain, and he followed it for half a league until it emerged in a wide green meadow, which at first appeared sickle-shaped, curving away from him; then, blinking in the late skylight, he saw that in fact it formed a ring around a clump of slender trees.

People were moving at random around the bases of these trees, where Thorinn saw a huddle of curious round structures of withy and vines. Up in the branches, a flash of movement caught his eye, and he saw platforms there with people on them.

As he approached, he found that some of the bulbous structures around the trees were little bowers; what he had taken for withies were simply the stalks of plants that had been bent together and secured with interlaced vines that still bore their leaves and blossoms. Children were squatting in a few of these. Other huts, somewhat larger, were covered almost to the ground by a solid green skin which, on examination, he found to be composed of broad leaves, overlapped and somehow sealed tightly together at their edges. Peering into the doorway of one of these, he saw heaped flowers and a few gourds; otherwise it was empty.

Voices piped behind him; the rest of the people were emerging from the trees. They crossed to the meadow, a few glancing at him but making no sign. They gathered around the base of the trees in little groups. A few disappeared into the green huts or climbed to the platforms above; then a few more. Thorinn, who had waited in vain for any invitation to follow them, withdrew a little and watched.

Now only two of the people remained, a woman and her little man. Arm in arm, they entered one of the green huts.

The birds in the treetops had fallen silent. Thorinn looked up. Silent and swift, an edge of darkness was sweeping across the sky. It was not high-arched, like the sky-scythe of Hovenskar, but straight as a string. In two heartbeats it had passed and the sky was dark.

Kneeling in the darkness, feeling the cool breeze that presently began to whisper across the meadow, Thorinn began to suspect that he was farther from home than he had reckoned.

4

How Thorinn roasted two fat waterfowl for his supper, and what happened thereafter.

Thorinn sat perched on a rock, chin in his hands, staring down at the smooth glassy curve of the water where it disappeared under the overhang. The voice in his head was a remote murmur, as steady and insistent as the water itself. The rocks below him were black and glistening with spray; the water made a subdued rushing sound, so constant and pervasive that it was like the sound of blood in his own veins. Twigs, then a broad leaf, rode down the shining back of the river, curved over and shot abruptly out of sight. He must go down, but he could not.

In three days he had followed the river from the western end of the valley, where it fell in a graceful cataract straight down the face of the mountain, to its exit here at the eastern end. He had crossed the river at the shallows, half a league above, and had followed the wall of mountains all the way around the valley. They were the same everywhere: sheer gray rock, unbroken, without a fissure, a ledge, a handhold. The mountains pierced the sky, or else

Something dark came into view and hung suspended in the middle of the disk. (p. 9)

. . . touched it to the sodden mass in the other half of the box. (p. 14)

In sick disgust he stepped into it. (p. 46)

He found rings, bracelets, ropes of jewels that spilled in a flood across the floor. (p. 52)

... the box was filled with a smooth bulge of glass or crystal in which he could see himself dimly reflected. (p. 53)

He struck something hard and was at rest in the heaving blackness. (p. 70)

. . . now one of the old ones came forward carrying the sword. (p. 86)

He . . . gripped the sky with one hand, and swung himself out. (p. 89)

the sky severed the mountains. There was no exit from the valley
except for the chasm into which the river fell.

The sky was dimming; it was time to think of supper, and then
a place to sleep.

He knew what he had tried so long to keep from knowing: the
mountains were not mountains, but walls of rock; the sky not a
sky, but the roof of a cavern. A fool might have known as much,
for he had traveled steadily downward from the Midworld . . .
but who could have believed that there were trees, a river, a sky
underground?

He went into the forest and picked fruit, but the sight and smell
of it made his stomach knot, and he threw it into the bushes.
Thinking of the water-fowl that nested along the riverbank, he
turned with sudden resolution. If nothing else, he could at least
hunt his own food and have a meal fit to eat.

The river was witchily green with reflected skylight among the
dark tussocks. Wading, he moved with caution, stopping at every
step to listen. A rustle from the clump ahead; as he plunged toward it, he heard a sleepy note and saw a crested head appear. He
got his hands on the warm feathered neck and wrung it, cutting off
the bird's sudden squawk. Another body thrashed up from the
grass, wings flapping; he lunged, got that one too. With the plump
bodies slung over his shoulder he waded ashore. Just as he
reached the bank, the night raced overhead and the world fell into
breathing blackness.

He searched the forest for fallen limbs, tore them loose from
the vines that clung to them with a thousand suckers, and kindled
a fire on the greensward, not far from the pod-vines. He plucked
and cleaned his two fowl—one was a cock, the other a young hen—
then contrived a spit between two forked branches thrust into the
ground, skewered his birds on it and roasted them over the fire.

A faint pattering began around him; a cool drop struck his
nose. Thorinn got a big leaf from the forest to cover the spit,
and another for himself. In the ruddy light, the greensward was
another place, walled in by darkness. Raindrops bombarded his
leaves and rebounded pale in the firelight. The crisp skin curled,
wept grease that sizzled in the flames; the smell that came from it
made his mouth fill with water, and he ate the first fowl with rag-
ing appetite before it was properly cool enough. Nothing had ever
tasted so good. He carried the second bird into the shelter of a

tree and ate a leg and a breast of it; then weariness overcame him;
he dropped the rest and stretched himself out. Rain rattled in the
leaves high overhead; beyond the lower branches, in the faint glow
of the fire, he saw it streaming coppery against the black air.

He was up at first light, washed in the river, then breakfasted on
the remains of the second bird. Lazy and replete, he lay down and
dozed again.

Some time later he woke with a start. Half a dozen of the older
children were staring at him across the ashes of his fire and the little heap of feathers, bones, and offal. Among them was the girl he
had spoken to before, or one like her. Their faces were white.

Questioning voices came from behind him; more people were
emerging from the forest. The children turned and ran toward
them, screaming as they went. A crowd formed around the children; it grew momentarily larger and noisier. Thorinn saw faces
turned toward him, staring eyes, open mouths.

Bewildered, he got up, but already the people were turning
away. Their voices dwindled; the whole crowd was moving back
into the forest. The last of them disappeared.

When he awoke the next morning, the presents he had given
them lay in a little heap at his side—pebbles, crystal, weasel's
skull, scrap of cloth.

Goryat's pride, which he had taught Thorinn, was in three
things only, never to turn his back on a foe, never to break an
oath, always to repay an injury. Beyond this Thorinn had no idea
of right and wrong, only a strong sense of justice and injustice. By
his lights he had done nothing that was either wrong or unjust; yet
it was obvious that he had somehow offended the people of the
cavern. They no longer came to the clearing by the river, or even
into the forest above it. At dusk on the seventh day, stealing down
the path to the village, he had spied on them from the trees and
had seen them coming back from the opposite direction, from
upriver, where they must have found a new playground. He dared
not show himself, for fear they would think he had polluted their
village as well by his presence.

The forest was changing. For half a league around the playground, leaves hung limp and shabby from the trees; fruits still
grew, but now the unripe ones were withered and hard, the rest
had a bloom of corruption and gave off a nauseous smell. He

began to detect the same changes in other places where he had slept and cooked his meals. He spent more and more of his time at the mouth of the river, staring at the smooth curve of the water as it fell over the lip.

He began to think of a boat, something made perhaps of the huge leaves the people used to build their huts. In his mind he saw himself floating down the current in such a boat, faster and faster . . . the cavern opens its mouth, the boat dives into darkness, then capsizes, and he struggles for breath in the roaring water.

No, a boat would not protect him; but what if he made two boats, and sealed them together like two halves of a nut, with himself inside? The idea aroused him, and he went into the forest for leaves of the proper size. He found them in profusion, and carried an armful down to the riverbank, but as he squatted turning them over, planning in his mind a framework of saplings on which the leaves could be stretched and gummed in place, he saw himself once more drifting down the current in his green shell . . . the boat strikes a rock, bursts open, the water floods in, and the man is struggling, drowning.

He cast the leaves aside, angry with himself and the gods, for it seemed to him that the answer was almost within his reach. Deep in thought as he wandered upriver, he found himself again at the deserted playground. He paused, looking up the slope, and his skin prickled. He went up to the forest's edge and stood before the pod-vine. Here like green thoughts hung the very things he had been imagining: they had been here all the time, yet he had not really seen them until now. The vine was still green and fresh; one pod hung heavy; the rest were invitingly open.

He tested an empty one by striking it repeatedly, first with a stick, then with a heavy stone. It resisted his blows; the outer shell of the pod was thick and resilient. He slashed it with his sword; even then, the tough fibers within held it together.

He imagined himself cutting a pod, taking it to the river where the current was swift, lying down inside it. . . . But would it close then, when he had cut it from its vine: and if it did, how was he to get the pod into the river?

Another, equally alarming thought: what if the water made the pod open? This, at least, he could find out by trial. He went back to the vine, grasped it above the closed pod, chopped at it with his sword. The blade rebounded at the first blow, then bit in; a milky sap oozed from the wound. Thorinn smote again, slashed the vine through.

The pod remained closed. Thorinn dragged it down the slope into the water, where it floated sluggishly among the reeds. He sat on a tussock and watched it. For a long time nothing happened. Bored and hungry, he got up and began to forage, coming back frequently to look at the floating pod. At last he found a nest of four speckled greenish eggs in one of the tussocks. He punctured one and sniffed it: it was strong-smelling but fresh. As he was tilting his head to drink the egg out of its shell, he heard a distant splash.

He turned. Nothing was to be seen, but from the direction of the pod came a thrashing sound in the water, then a choked cry. Thorinn dropped the egg and hurried. Before he could reach the spot, he saw a human form flounder upright among the reeds.

It was the boy. He stared wildly at Thorinn, then whirled and tried to run. He fell almost at once in the shallows, but was up again and struggling to the shore. Thorinn saw him reeling up the slope; at the forest's edge, he turned a white face for an instant.

Thorinn found the pod awash among the reeds. It was open and full of water; the soft pink inner surface was already swelling and slimy to the touch.

He knew, then, that the pod would remain closed long enough to carry him down the river, and then release him; but the problem of getting himself into the pod, then the pod into the river, was still unsolved.

Except for this, his plans were complete. He had found the place, a steep grassy bank on the far side of the river, where the water was deep and swift. Nearby in the forest was a healthy podvine. When he was ready, he had only to cut a pod, take it to the bank . . . and then what? He saw himself getting in, the pod sliding as it slowly closed around him; the pod splashes into the river, not yet fully closed; water enters it, then it closes: and the man inside, as the pod darts down the current—is he drowning, asleep, helpless?

Or, on a gentler slope: the pod moves more slowly, closes before it reaches the brink, then catches, halts. It lies there on the bank above the river. If it does not go into the river, will it ever open?

Another day passed while he turned the problem over again and again. The rotting forest was turning black and sending out clouds of stench for half a league around the deserted playground. The waterfowl had abandoned that part of the river.

Returning to the place he had chosen, he found that the sickness had started there. The grass was turning yellow, brown at the tips. His hesitation ended. He went to the vine in the forest, found it still healthy. He cut a pod, taking care to get a good length of vine with it. Still without knowing what he meant to do, he dragged it back to the riverbank and laid it on the slope. Below, the water rushed smoothly by. He tossed in a dry twig, watched it dart away out of sight.

He was lightheaded with fasting. He thought, if water flowed here on the ground, it would wash the pod down into the river. But water ran in its own fashion. The river raced below him, cold and swift.

Or fire: if he could tie the vine to a tree, perhaps by a smaller vine, then build a fire under it to burn through the vine. . . . But what if the fire went out; or what if it spread in the dry grass, and reached the pod before it burned through the vine?

Then he saw the answer in its simplicity. He went into the forest again, cut down a tough, thin creeper and trimmed it to a single length of half a dozen ells. The creeper was strong: he could not break it in his hands.

Some dry yellow gourds caught his eye; one was nearly two ells long. He cut it from the vine; it was light and hollow; seeds rattled inside it. He imagined the gourd tied to one end of the creeper, the pod to the other, the creeper passing from one to the other around a stake or sapling. The pod, with himself inside it, would be heavier, it would pull the gourd around the stake and both would fall into the river. But if the gourd were full of water. . . .

Kneeling on the riverbank, he cut a large hole near the stem of the gourd, then thrust it underwater and held it until the last of the air bubbled out. He raised the slippery thing with difficulty; it weighed as much as he did.

He laid the gourd down, careful not to spill it, and traced with his eye the way the line should run, from the gourd to a stake driven into the ground, then down to the pod. He saw himself puncturing the gourd, the water dribbling out. Thorinn lies down in the pod, which closes over him. At length the gourd, growing lighter, glides up the slope; the pod, moving down, keeps the line taut; the gourd reaches the stake. . . .

But the stake should not be there. It might catch the curved neck of the gourd, the creeper knotted around it, the knobby surface of the gourd itself. Yet the stake must be there in the first place, to hold the pod.

Dissatisfied, he thought of a moveable peg, a wooden hook. He searched among the dead branches in the forest, found a forked limb with a projecting stub that was smooth and no bigger than his thumb. He held the limb this way and that: tilted up, the stub would hold the loop of cord; tilt it down, and the cord would slide off freely. But how to make it tilt? Suddenly, in his mind, gourd, forked limb, cord all came together, and he knew.

He dropped the forked limb near the gourd and went back into the forest. Half-buried in the undergrowth was a bigger limb, three ells long and as thick as his thigh. With much toil he dragged it out and set it crossways on the slope, wedging the ends behind a shrub and a stone. The smaller limb he set with its stem on the log, the forked ends on the slope above it. The projecting stub stood straight up. Now he carried the heavy gourd up behind the log and laid it down, with care, in the embrace of the forked branch. With a length of creeper he lashed the gourd securely to the branch. He picked up the rest of the creeper, made a loop in one end, slipped it over the smooth projecting stub, and leaned back with all his weight. The gourd did not move.

He tied the other end of the creeper to the pod-vine, then placed the pod directly below the log, within an ell of the bank over the river. He examined his work again, and saw that it was good. The water would run out of the punctured gourd, its weight would lessen; the greater weight of the pod would drag it forward, the forked limb would tilt, the cord would slip off the stub.

All that remained was to do it. Thorinn slowly put on his garments, made sure that all his possessions were in the wallet, sheathed his sword. The pink, soft pod-halves gaped open. Below him he could hear the unending rush of the water.

Once more he examined every part of the engine he had made. He knelt behind the log, looked at the heavy-bellied curve of the gourd between the forks of the limb. He drew his sword, set the point against the bottom of the gourd, then hesitated. He found himself thinking of other ways, of somehow ascending the cataract at the other end of the valley, or finding the doorway in the sky. . . .

Go down, said the voice in his mind, and he thrust the sword in. Water spurted; when he withdrew the blade, a thin stream ran from the gash, twisting as it went, rebounding in lazy droplets from the turf below.

Thorinn got up and went down the slope to the waiting pod. Its pink halves gaped in invitation. In sick disgust, he stepped into it, felt it loathsomely soft under his feet. His muscles jumped with the desire to get away from it, but he made himself sit down, then lie back in the pod's fleshy embrace. He saw a narrowing strip of sky, then the podflesh came slowly and smotheringly against his face. The rush of the water below faded to silence. He struggled to get out, and found it quite easy. The pod turned to mist, and he was free under a curious twilit sky, walking without fear in a land where interesting things were happening, and where friendly people, whose faces he could not quite see, were speaking to him in words he almost seemed to understand. He realized that he had lost his sword, and that alarmed him faintly, but when he looked again it was there, bright and shining at his waist. Then he realized it was gone again, but it did not seem to matter. The things that were happening and the things said to him were so interesting and pleasant that years went by in this way without any weariness, and it seemed to him that he could well congratulate himself on having attained this mode of life, so much better in every way than the other; and he pitied those who were still groaning with toil in that former life. He mentioned this to one or two of his companions, and they agreed entirely; he knew this by their voices, although their words never became entirely clear. Then after a long time something unpleasant began to happen. It came to him from a direction in which he could not defend himself, nor could the others help him. It had no face or meaning, but he could not ignore it; it receded, then it came back again, more brutally demanding than ever. He saw that something could be done, but it would mean giving up all his ease and pleasure to the end of time, and while he hesitated, the thing came back once more, and now it had a sound: the roar of water.

5

How Thorinn entered a treasure cave and found a magic box that could speak, albeit foolishly.

2957 A.D.:

In this yer the wyse men forwiste that er 50 yer be paced our Sonne wolde brenne so breme that hit wolde roste us all lyk mete in a forneys, and wolde be our bane.

Than spake som and seyde: "Maken we a char of this our Erthe; so shal we flee our Sonnes fyr and seke another sterre."

Yet others answerde: "So eek shal we lese our eir, for hit wol frese, but that we wirken a greet roofe overthwart the world: and of which matere wirken we swich a roofe, that of hits owen wighte hit ne shal falle?"

Than sterted oon that seyde: "Wirken we a blader fulfild of eir! So shal our roofe kepe eir, whyl eir kepe eek the roofe!"

So they bigane, and swinkede ful 20 yer in this werke.

Water stung his eyes, his nose. The roaring blackness whirled around him. He struggled against it, but his body was like a stone. Water surged over his face again. Half strangled, he struck out,

and found the soft edges of the pod under his hands. His eyes
were open but he could see nothing. The pod tilted, shuddered;
the roaring of the water was beneath him. He floundered, trying to
turn over; the pod tilted and he felt the black water sucking at his
legs. He strained to pull himself against the pod. It was canted,
half out of the water. The water roared black beneath it, trying to
drag him down.

He struck out with his feet, touched slippery stone, then lost it.
It seemed to him that the pod was jammed against some crevice
down which the water was pouring. He groped again, found footing once more, but the pod swung and he was kicking in the water
again.

He worked his grasp higher on the pod, fighting the tug of the
water. He was shaking with cold. Here the pod narrowed; he was
able to get one arm under it, grasp it from the opposite side.
Hanging underneath in this way, he put his foot back, touched
bottom, and braced himself precariously. The current streamed
against the back of his legs. He turned clumsily, one hand on the
pod. The pod began to swing; letting it go, he leaped. The water
swept his legs out from under him and he was down, pawing the
slippery stone underwater. He fell, was swept back, struggled up,
fell again. Something smote him on the cheek, making his head
ring; he grabbed, found himself clinging to a massive stone half
out of water. He dragged himself across it, braced himself on the
far side. Only then could he pause to cough the water out of his
throat.

The blackness was solid and velvety; the rushing roar of the
water never stopped. He began to remember now, and understood
that the pod had carried him down the cataract. He was safe for
the moment and not drowning, and that was all he cared about.

After a time he roused himself enough to make sure that he still
had his sword and wallet, and then to fumble in the wallet for his
light-box. He uncapped the box, and a pale beam sprang out.

In its light, he saw the cold water silvery around him. Only two
ells off, the pod slowly turned in a whirlpool; all his struggle had
been to come that little way. The ragged ceiling was close overhead. Below, the water was everywhere; he could see no end to it.
A few irregular blocks of stone rose above the water or could be
seen dimly shining beneath it; they looked as if they had fallen
from the broken ceiling.

Moving from one stone to the next, supporting himself with one hand and holding the light-box with the other, he put the whirlpool behind him. He saw another in the distance and avoided it; then he noticed that the water was growing shallower. The stone under his feet was broken and tilted, this way and that. It rose until he was wading in sluggish water, no more than ankle-deep.

Ahead he saw a line of brightness where the water curled over the edge of a hole. As he approached, he felt a cool breath. He looked down over the lip. Below he saw broken stone, jeweled with the rebounding slow droplets of the water that fell on it.

Lying full length in the water, he put his head and one arm down, turning the light-box this way and that. He could see nothing but darkness beyond the ragged curtains of water. He could not tell where the falling water ran away. The slabs between were almost dry.

He stood, hesitated a moment, then stepped off, pointing the light-box down as he fell. He landed on a tilted slab, lost his footing, and sat down hard, but without taking any hurt.

Now the roar of the water was muted overhead, and he could hear the gurgle of lesser streams running away somewhere below. The falling curtains of water were all around him, ghostly silver, pricked with the jewels of floating droplets. Drifting water-points burst on his skin with tiny cool kisses.

There were gaps in the falling curtains, torn by the irregular stone above. He put his head through the widest of these openings, saw other broken slabs, other curtains of water beyond.

Following the cool air, he made his way among the gray and silver curtains that hung everywhere from the ceiling. Rivulets ran toward him underfoot among the slabs of stone, and he knew by this that the floor was slanting upward. At length the falling curtains of water grew less numerous, and the sound diminished to a mournful pattering behind him. Ahead, the cavern broke into a tortured complexity of shapes in which he found a narrow passage leading upward. He paused to tip out the water from his wallet and to dry his hair as well as he could with his hands; then he followed the passage. It coiled away ahead of him, always upward, always rounded, irregular, dry, and empty in the glow of his light-box.

At length the passage widened into a greater darkness. Thorinn stepped out into it cautiously, found himself in a narrow cavern half-choked with a pile of fallen stones. Beyond, in the far wall, he saw a jagged opening.

He climbed the heap of stones and peered in. Light glimmered back from objects whose forms he could not make out. A breath of air came from the opening, but it was slow and stale. He hesitated a moment, then climbed through the gap in the wall and dropped to the level floor below.

Silence pressed in upon his ears, a silence more profound even than that of the passage behind him. On every side stood massive objects piled one on another, with slender rods between them. The floor he stood on was perfectly level and as smooth as ice. It was not stone, but some gray, greasy material which seemed faintly warm to the touch. The air was dry and warm. The huge columns stood in rows; their tops disappeared in the darkness.

Thorinn moved between the columns, touching them curiously as he passed. The rods, of cold metal, supported racks on which were piled bundles and bales, and other things for which Thorinn had no names, all covered with some cool, water-smooth substance. He began to realize that he must be in some troll's storehouse, and he paused, listening; but the silence was unbroken.

He slid his hands curiously around one of the bundles. It was so smooth and heavy that it was hard to find any purchase on it, but he dragged it out at last and lowered it to the floor. It was almost as broad as his arms could span, vaguely oblong but with all its corners rounded, like a huge gray cheese. He looked in vain for any seam or opening; the smooth surface was unbroken.

Next he tried to cut it with his sword. At the first touch, the covering opened like a mouth. Thorinn put his fingers under the edges, marveling at the thinness and transparency of the stuff, finer than the skin of an onion. He pulled, and the tear lengthened easily. The covering split and tore without resistance, and he peeled it off in great rustling sheets. Underneath was a gray soft substance like bread dough; he could push it in, but the hollow filled out again at once, nor could he tear it with his fingers.

Again he used the sword. The gray stuff cut readily, but would not tear like the other. When he pried at the gash he had made, sticky-looking fibers at the bottom clung stubbornly together. He slashed deeper, and at last it gave way, opening in a slit as the transparent stuff had done, and he saw something else beneath it: a gleam of russet and gold.

He tore away the gray substance in lumps, threw them aside. In the glow of his light-box, a bundle of stuff lay revealed, and he caught his breath. Rich and soft beyond belief it was, russet and gold and scarlet in shimmering patterns that were not printed on the fabric but woven into it. He unfolded and unwrapped the cloth, spreading it out on the floor as it went; it covered the whole width of the aisle, and still there was more. Thorinn dropped it and stared at it in wonder. Such a piece of stuff was beyond price; he could ask what he liked for it. This one bale had made him rich. And all the others?

He attacked a second bundle, found it contained another cloth like the first, colored in deep purple, royal blue, peacock green. In a fury of excitement, he ran to the next aisle, found a rack of smaller bundles, some of which, no bigger than his head, had fallen to the floor. He chose one, slashed it open. Inside was a glittering device of brass and ebony, evidently a magical instrument. Such things, he knew, could injure any man not schooled in their use, and he laid it respectfully aside.

The next was a pretty jug with a handle and a spout to pour from. He tilted it to see why it was so heavy, but only a single drop of moisture came out.

The next was a black-and-red-patterned box in which, nested in purple velvet, lay dozens of tiny bright figurines of men and ladies.

Stunned with joy, he ran to the next aisle and found other magical engines. The next: Yen-metal knives smaller than his finger, with tiny blades as sharp as his sword. The next: hammers, wedges, no bigger than the knives, and other tiny tools whose use he could not imagine.

The fever to open more and yet more bundles made him forget weariness, cold, thirst, and hunger. He found clothing—wide-skirted robes, heavy with brocade; tunics and breeks of gossamer stuff; shoes, marvelously thin and supple. He found rings, bracelets, ropes of jewels that spilled in a flood across the floor. Riches piled up around him, and still he knew that he had barely begun.

Once he paused long enough to gather all his trove into one place, and sorting through it, try to decide what he would take with him. Then the blank gray faces of the unopened parcels drove him to frenzy again, and against all common sense he attacked bundles larger than any he had yet opened, gray oblongs taller than himself, ripping open their fronts without removing them from the racks, merely to see what was inside. (Cabinets of polished wood inlaid with nacre. Huge engines of metal and glass. Chairs with arms curved like serpents. More bales of cloth, ten times larger than the others.)

Then for weariness alone he forebore, and sat with his head on his heavy arms. Hunger and thirst returned. He tipped up his wallet and drank what little water was in it, but it was not enough. He began to think of finding some container and going back through the caverns for water. The wallet would do, but he wanted to keep that dry to hold his treasures. He could put some of the smallest things in it, the jewels perhaps, and make a bundle of the rest to carry on his back.

He remembered the jug, and looked for it: there it was, at the edge of the great pile he had made. When he took it up, it seemed to him that it was heavier than before. He shook it, and it gurgled. Without thinking, he tipped it over. Water splashed on his feet.

Thorinn righted the jug and stared at it. He shook it again, and it gurgled. He put the spout cautiously to his lips, tilted it up, tasted. It was water, cold and pure, as good as the spring water of Hovenskar. He put his head back and drank in great gulps until the jug was empty.

To make sure, he held it upside down. A single drop fell, then another, then none. He put the jug down, sat by it and watched it awhile, but nothing happened. He picked it up, turned it over: water ran out, a thin stream that stopped almost at once. But how could there be any, when the jug had been dry a few moments ago?

Resolved to wait longer this time, he turned his back on the jug and opened another bundle. This yielded a black box with rounded edges, one edge thicker than the others. It had no lid; it was open but not empty: the box was filled with a smooth bulge of glass or crystal in which he could see himself dimly reflected. If it was a mirror, it was a poor one. Down another aisle, he found many small bundles; he took one and opened it. Inside the nest of gray dough-stuff there were dozens of little boxes with bright markings on them, green, violet, yellow, red. He found the trick of opening them—you put your thumbnail under one edge of the lid, and the box sprang apart. Inside was an oblong piece of some cheesy substance. Thorinn sniffed it, then tore off a crumb and tasted it incredulously. It *was* cheese—bland, with an unfamiliar flavor, but cheese all the same. He ate the whole piece in two bites, then opened another box, and another, and ate until he was full. Weariness forgotten, he carried the rest of the boxes back to his treasure heap.

He picked up the little jug; it gurgled. He could not see inside it very well, but it seemed to be at least half full. He drank again, more out of curiosity than thirst, and sat down with his back against one of the bales of cloth. The black box lay nearby on the floor; Thorinn lazily reached for it with his foot and hooked it nearer. It slid, checked on some irregularity in the floor, then tipped forward on its heavy edge and stood upright. Inside, the crystal seemed to flicker with colored light for an instant.

"Here, that's odd," said Thorinn, sitting up.

The box flickered again, and a voice spoke.

Thorinn was on his feet without knowing how he had got there. His sword was in his hand. He whirled, looked this way and that, then circled the heap of treasure and peered behind the columns, looked down the aisles. He listened, heard nothing.

He went back to the box and stared at it dubiously. "Was that you?" he demanded.

The voice spoke again, incomprehensibly. It was a quiet voice, calm and measured.

"Are you in there?" Thorinn asked, stooping to peer into the box. The voice replied. The dark crystal lighted up. Thorinn saw a confused pattern of light and shadow; then part of it moved, and he saw a tiny crouching figure, dressed in stained leather, with a sword in its hand. When he moved, it moved.

"Is that *me?*" he cried.

The voice said, "That me?"

Thorinn looked at the box with deep distrust, withdrew a little and sat down facing it. The crystal had gone dark; now it lighted up again, and he was looking as if down a tunnel at the same tiny figure, with a column of stacked bundles behind it. It was like looking at oneself in a mirror of ice. Yet when he raised his sword in his right hand, the figure raised the sword in its right hand, not its left, as in a proper mirror.

"You," said the voice.

"Yes, it's me," Thorinn replied. "How do you do that?"

The crystal went dark. "How do me do that?" said the voice.

"Yes, how do you?" asked Thorinn impatiently. "What's the matter? Why do you talk that way?"

"Why do me talk that way?"

Thorinn felt baffled. "Yes, why do you talk that way?"

The crystal lighted again. "You talk."

"Well, I know I talk. I talk much better than you."

In the crystal, the tiny figure seemed to rush forward without moving until its face filled the box. Thorinn fell silent, but in the box he saw his own lips moving. "You talk?" asked the voice. The face rushed forward again, and now he saw only the mouth and chin. "You talk?"

Convinced now that he had to do with some harmless and rather stupid spirit, Thorinn said, "Yes, I talk," and gesturing toward his own mouth, he spoke with exaggerated clarity, opening his mouth wide with each word. "I—talk. Talk. You understand?"

"Talk," said the voice. "I understand." The crystal darkened, lighted again, and Thorinn saw a hand. It was his own hand, but when he moved his hand, the hand in the box did not move. "That's my hand," he said.

"That's my hand."

"No, not yours—it's my hand."

"That's your hand."

"I said so, didn't I?"

"You said so. Talk." In the crystal, now he saw only one finger; the rest of the hand had turned all misty.

"That's my finger."

"That's your finger. Talk." Now he saw his thumb, and he told the voice what that was called; and then his arm, his leg, his foot, his toes, his head, his ears, his eyes, and so on until he lost patience and stood up. "You ask too many questions," he said.

"You ask."

"All right, who are you? How did you get in that box?"

"Box?"

Thorinn squatted, touched the box. "This thing. This box. How did you get in there?"

The crystal lighted, and he was looking at the box: a box inside the box. The box inside was not lighted, and it stood on a yellow surface. "This box," said the voice.

"Yes, the box. How did you get inside it?"

"I are this box. Talk." The crystal glowed, and Thorinn saw a

man in stiff scarlet robes, with a shimmer of green and gold behind him. "That's a man. He must be rich."

The man disappeared, and he saw a woman with fair hair,
dressed in similar robes. "That's a woman. Is it his wife?"

So they went on, and Thorinn told the box what a boy was
called, a girl, a tree, a leaf, a branch; but sometimes the box
showed him engines or other shapes he had never seen before, and
he would say, "What's that?" or "I don't know what that is." At
last his head began to droop, and the pictures in the box grew so
blurred that he could not make them out at all. "Talk," said the
box. His head came up with a painful jerk, and he realized that he
had been asleep for an instant.

"No more talk," he said thickly. "Good night." The box said
nothing. Thorinn rolled over onto a pile of folded cloth, pulled an
edge of it over him, and was instantly asleep.

When he awoke, he had forgotten all that had happened, and at
first he did not know where he was. Then joy filled him when he
saw his treasures. He pottered about among them for a while, examining this and that. If only he could get all this back to the
Midworld, or even the thousandth part of it! Thinking deeply, he
crawled through the opening in the wall to ease himself outside;
came back and opened one of the boxes of cheese for his break-
fast.

The box was silent and dark; it had said nothing since he had
awakened, and that was odd, since it had been so garrulous before.

"Box, are you there?"

The crystal lighted. "I am here."

"Tell me, box, what is above this cave?"

"What is this cave?"

"This cave," Thorinn said, waving his arms. "This place here,
where we are. What is above it?" He pointed upward as he spoke.

In the crystal, a brightly lighted little hollow shape appeared: it
was like a long empty box with walls of glass. At one end of it
there was a hollow worm: that must be the passage by which
Thorinn had entered. Near the other end, a tiny thread connected
the cave to a much larger tunnel above.

"Show me where that goes," said Thorinn, pointing.

In the crystal, the box-shape dwindled, receding, while more of the tunnel appeared. Presently the tunnel crossed a shaft as big as itself.

"And that? Where does it go?"

The picture shrank again; now he could see that the shaft met another tunnel, and above that the dark background ended.

"Is that the Midworld?"

"What is the Midworld?"

"The top of the earth, where there are no more caves."

"That is the Midworld."

Thorinn pointed again. "How far is it from here to the top?"

"What is how far?"

"How *far*," Thorinn said, waving his arms by way of explanation. "How many ells?"

"What are ells?"

Thorinn sat down on the floor and stared at the box in exasperation. "Ells are—well, anybody knows that. Ells are how long something is." He spread his hands apart. "This is an ell."

The box said, "How long are you?"

"You mean how tall. Two ells. I'm two ells tall."

In the crystal, two yellow marks appeared. "How many?"

"Two."

One of the marks vanished. "How many?"

"One."

Two more appeared. "How many?"

"Three."

Another mark. "How many?"

"Four."

The box, Thorinn realized, did not even know how to count.

So they went on until they got to twenty-one, and then the box said, "Two tens are twenty?"

"Yes, that's right, and three tens are thirty."

"And four tens?"

"Four tens are forty. Five tens are fifty, six tens are sixty." At a hundred and ten, the box stopped him again.

"Twenty tens are two hundred?"

"Yes."

"It is three hundred and thirty-two ells from here to the top."

Thorinn sat awhile with his chin on his fist. The geas had never prevented him from going up when there was no other way to go; therefore he could surely get into the tunnel. Then, if he could but

gain the Midworld, though the geas would be on him still, he need
only keep away from pits and chasms, for no magic could make a
man go down through the solid earth. But he could never climb
that shaft against the geas; and the geas could be removed only by
its maker, or by a greater magician.

Struck by a thought, he said, "Box, can you do magic?"

"What is magic?"

"Magic is—well, for instance, a spell that makes something
happen."

"What is a spell?"

"Well, suppose you want to find something." Thorinn picked
up two jewels from the heap, a red one and a green; he tossed the
red one over his shoulder, hearing it click and roll down the aisle.
Then he picked up the green one and chanted three times,
"Brother, find your brother." He threw the green jewel, marking
where it went. When he found it, it lay beside the red one.

"You see, that was a spell—I found the red one by making the
green one go to the same place."

"Not the spell. You found the red one."

Incredulous, Thorinn tried to explain again, but the box insisted
that it knew nothing of spells, and he gave up. Perhaps the magician who had made the box had taken care to teach it no magic,
for fear it would become greater than himself.

At any rate, why should he not attempt some magic of his own?
Many times he had watched Goryat casting spells to keep wolves
away, or to make sure the mares would come fresh in the spring
and the foals be born alive. Supposing his spell worked but
poorly, or that it lasted only a short time, still it might be enough
for his purpose. He brooded over this awhile, then set aside certain articles from the heap—a tiny figurine of an old bearded man,
who reminded him somewhat of Goryat; slender bits of wood
painted with designs in red; a box full of a fine gray powder.
These he wrapped carefully and put away in his wallet. Then he
began to consider what else he could take and what he must leave
behind.

The magic jug was a problem. He thought of hanging it from
his belt, but that would be awkward, and unless he could contrive
some sort of cover for it, the jug would be spilling water down his
leg; whereas if he put it in his wallet, it would take up too much

room. He could fill the jug with jewels, but then would the water run over?

He remembered that when he had first taken the jug from its wrapping, there had been no water in it, or at any rate only a drop. Was it being wrapped up that made the difference? He cut a piece of the transparent stuff, wrapped it around the jug after pouring the water out, and tied it tightly with strips of the same material. Later, when he came back from a trip to gather food, he opened it and it was still dry. He filled it to the brim with jewels, wrapped it again and put it in his wallet.

The next thing was to be sure he knew how to find the exit from the cavern.

"Box, show me this cave again."

The crystal lighted; the same bright hollow shape appeared.

"How far is it from here to the hole in the roof?"

A short yellow line appeared across the width of the cavern. "It is two hundred and ninety-one ells—" A longer line, lengthwise, almost to the end. "—and eight hundred and thirty-eight ells."

"Eight *hundred* ells? How big is this cave?"

"It is eight hundred and fifty ells long, and fifteen ells tall, and three hundred and nineteen ells—"

"Three hundred and nineteen ells wide?"

"Yes, three hundred and nineteen ells wide."

Thorinn was silent in amazement. "Is it all like this—all full of things?"

"It is all full of things."

Thorinn tried to imagine that, and could not. "Box, who made this cave?"

"What is made?"

Thorinn tried to explain, and grew hot-faced with exasperation. "Well, look here," he said finally, and picked up his light-box. "I made this box. I cut these pieces of wood and glued them together, and I fitted the pieces of mica in here at the ends—well, one of them is gone now, I lost it in the river. Then I made the lid and put it on here, and then the box was made, you see. I made it."

In the crystal, an image of Thorinn appeared, fitting little pieces of wood together. It was over in a moment, and the figure held a light-box in its hand.

"You made this box?"

"That's right. Now who made all this? Who made you?"

"A box made me."

"You mean you made yourself?"

"I mean I made me?"

"Well, did you?"

"A box made this box." In the crystal appeared a huge black engine, out of the end of which, one after another, were dropping little black boxes, each with a glint of crystal inside it. They floated away out of sight; it made Thorinn dizzy to watch them.

"You mean an engine. An engine made you—and all these other things?"

"Engines made me and all these other things."

"Well, but who made the engines?"

"Engines made the engines."

Thorinn gave it up. He made the box show him the picture of the cave again, then what was around it. In the new picture, the cave was a tiny bright shape at the top, while all around it other transparent passages ran off in every direction, some twisting, some straight, leading to other caverns. His idea had been to make sure there was no better way up to the Midworld than the one the box had showed him before, but as he asked the box to show him more and still more, he grew fascinated by the maze of passages, caverns, and shafts crisscrossing each other; there seemed to be no end to it. New lines kept floating into the picture while the old ones grew smaller and closer together. "How did it ever come to be like that?" he asked. "The whole Underworld?"

In the crystal, the network of lines vanished and a man's face appeared, brown and smiling; at least Thorinn supposed he was a man, though he was beardless. His black hair was cut short and combed back, exposing his ears and forehead. His lips moved. After a moment the box said, "This is the world." Behind the brown-faced man a big green and blue mottled ball was floating against a background of darkness. The man's lips went on moving, but no sound came. The ball receded, grew very small.

"What is he saying?" Thorinn asked. "Let me hear what he says."

Now the man himself began speaking, but it was gibberish; Thorinn could not understand a word. The ball was tiny now, and to one side of it, over the man's head, a dot of yellow light ap-

peared. It grew slowly; suddenly it was very big and bright, and
Thorinn could see flames leaping from its surface.

Then it all vanished, and instead he was looking at a green
landscape dotted with men and women who were all standing
looking up at something huge and flat and silvery that was receding slowly overhead, as if somehow they had brought the sky
down, then raised it again. The man's voice was still speaking, but
Thorinn could not see him. Now the sky was high overhead,
where it belonged, and little dark engines were moving across it.

Then they were underground, watching a huge engine that ate
its way into the solid rock, leaving a bright round tunnel behind.
Then there were scenes of great caverns full of engines and people, and floating egg-shaped things that crossed the caverns and
darted along tunnels, up and down shafts, all brightly lit, shining. . . . Then the brown man again, and behind him a picture
like the drawing of the Underworld the box had showed him before, only that it was circular, with many rings one inside the
other, and four straight lines radiating from the smallest circle of
all, in the center. Then the circle changed into a ball again; this
time it was white. Watching these pictures made Thorinn uneasy
in a way he could not understand; it was like being afraid, and because there was nothing to be afraid of, that made him angry. The
brown man was still speaking, the yellow point of light had appeared, and the silvery ball, shrunken to a dot, was crawling away
toward a cloud of other bright dots. Now the other dots swung,
came closer, darting forward like frostflakes in a storm until only
one hung in the center of the crystal, growing larger and brighter.

"That's enough," Thorinn said. The crystal went dark. He had
been watching so long that he had grown thirsty again, and had to
unwrap the jug, let it fill, drink, and then wrap it up again.

The smallest piece of cloth he had was far too bulky to carry,
but he cut off a strip an ell wide and as long as he was tall. He
spread this on the floor and rolled up his cheeseboxes and other
things in it—clothing, shoes, the little figurines, tools and knives,
the talking box, some leftover jewels—turning the ends in as he
went. He did this twice over before he had the roll packed to his
liking, with the heavier things in the middle, the food outside
where it could be easily reached. He tied it with strips of cloth,
and cut other strips to make loops which would fit over his
shoulders.

He changed the moss in his light-box, shouldered his burdens, and set off past the ends of the aisles, counting his paces. The tall columns marched past him with their heads buried in the darkness. Here and there small parcels had been knocked to the floor, and he conjectured that the earth-shock must have done that, when Snorri began to rumble; probably that was the cause, too, of the gap in the wall through which he had entered. Before that, the cavern must have been sealed up . . . how long?

When he had gone two hundred and ninety ells, he turned down the nearest aisle and began counting his paces again. The endless ranks of columns moved past him in the glow of the light-box. When he paused to listen, there was no sound. When he had gone eight hundred and forty ells, a gray wall loomed up ahead: he had reached the end of the cavern. He swung himself up onto the nearest rack and began to climb it.

The bottoms of the stacks disappeared; he was climbing in the fitful glow of his light-box with darkness all around. In the silence, the rack with its gray bundles seemed to glide downward past his body, as if he were not climbing at all but hanging in midair and pulling down more and more of an endless metal serpent. In a few moments he saw a dim gray reflection overhead. It was the ceiling, and when he stood on top of the stack a moment later he could reach up and touch it with his hands. He could see the tops of other stacks to left and right, gray hummocks rising out of the darkness, but there was no sign of any opening in the roof of the cave.

He turned away from the cavern wall, leaped to the next stack, then to the next, examining the ceiling from each. When he had traversed ten stacks in this way, he leaped the aisle to the next row and began working back along it, meaning to trace a path around and around the original ten stacks, like a man winding string on a twig, until he found the opening; but he had hardly begun his second cast when it appeared, off to his left: a round black hole in the ceiling.

The shaft was circular and three spans wide, like the one that had led him into the cavern he had mistaken for the Midworld. Standing under it and stretching up his arm with the light-box, he thought he could even make out a brownish something that might be a shield closing it at the top.

When he stood on his toes, he could just get his hands onto the smooth walls of the shaft; but that was no matter. He planted himself directly under the opening, bent his knees, leaped. As he shot up into the opening, he put out his arms and knees, braced himself, came to rest. A thrust and a wriggle, and he was half an ell farther up; now he could support himself with hands and one foot against one side, back against the other. Hampered a little by the bundle across his shoulders, he was still able to climb rapidly enough. In a few moments his head was touching the brown hollow disk that closed the shaft. He touched it, and it swung aside; a black cusp widened to a circle. He was up, through it into darkness that turned suddenly to a flicker of pale light.

As those vast arching shapes exploded around him in a kind of silent sizzling, Thorinn flattened himself to the floor. The cold shield was under his hand; he slapped it, felt it swing, felt the cool upward breath, then the shaft walls were burning his hands and knees as he braked his fall; the shield swung over his head and the light was gone.

With pounding heart, Thorinn hung in the shaft and stared upward. There was no sound. He tried to remember what he had seen: vast arcs of light that swooped up flickering into the darkness. . . . What could it have been? He held himself ready to let go and drop instantly, if the shield should begin to turn; but nothing happened. At last he climbed the shaft again.

He put his hand on the shield, turned it carefully. A lozenge of darkness appeared; there was no sound, no scent of danger. Thorinn widened the opening until it was black and round above him. With painstaking caution he thrust his head up; then, bracing himself to hold the shield open, he raised his arm with the lightbox. Darkness. He raised himself a little, head and shoulders through the opening; and a sudden flicker burst almost under his chin, ran away swooping and shimmering upward in multiple arcs. . . .

When he ducked his head, the flickering died; darkness returned. He raised himself again. The lights sprang up, flickering, swooping far overhead. They steadied, burned clear and cold. Thorinn raised himself a little more, cautiously, then still more, and climbed out.

He was standing at the bottom of a vast tunnel whose walls curved up to become the ceiling an incredible distance overhead. The lines of light ringed it; the nearest of these, only an ell away,

was a white ribbon that curved up, up, growing thinner until it was
no more than a bright thread above. On either side of it were
others, set three ells apart. In one direction they were dazzling
bright, in the other much dimmer and more diffuse; he counted
twenty of each. The reason for the difference, he saw, was that the
rings were lighted only on one side, so that in one direction he saw
not the lights themselves but their reflections in the tunnel wall. As
he looked down the tunnel, the farthest rings were perfect upright
circles, but those nearer to him grew fatter at the bottom until
they were vast egg-shapes that leaned together overhead.

He was trembling with awe; why had the box not made him understand how huge these tunnels were? He felt himself tiny and
exposed; the distant rings were like giants' eyes staring. He
glanced at the closed shield in the floor, then leaned to examine
the nearest ring more closely. The floor was made of some
smooth, hard substance; embedded in it, the ring stood up two
spans high, hollow on the bright side, flat on the other, with a flat
dark edge the breadth of his hand. He touched the dark surface
cautiously, then the bright: one was as cool as the other.

He hopped over it and took a stride toward the next ring. Far
down at the black end of the tunnel there was a flicker: a new ring
inside the others. Thorinn stared at it. Something was wrong. He
turned, counting the bright rings, and there were still twenty.

He began to hop in long floating strides down the middle of the
tunnel. Each time he soared over one of the rings, a new one appeared ahead; the eye of blackness at the end of the tunnel remained always the same. He thought of the pictures in the box,
and of the egg-shaped things that darted along the tunnels, up and
down the giant shafts. And did the lights follow them wherever
they went, so that where they were, there was light, and when they
had passed, the tunnel waited in darkness?

He began to move faster, in order to see the bright rings run on
ahead. A kind of exhilaration took him, and he ran faster and
faster, as if he could catch the fleeing rings of light. The tunnel
slipped by him in deathly silence, and again he began to feel that
he was not moving at all, but posturing motionless in the air while
the illusory tunnel flowed past him, out of one nothingness into
another.

Without warning, the black eye at the end of the tunnel flared
bright. Thorinn stumbled to a halt. What had been a black disk an

instant ago was now a globe of light, striped with faint dark lines as if it were a spinning top, and for a moment the illusion was so strong that he almost turned to flee, certain that the monstrous globe, which filled the tunnel, was whirling down upon him. Then he saw that it was not bulging, but hollow: he was looking through the end of the tunnel into some vast lighted space beyond.

As he approached, the last ring of the tunnel grew enormous around him, and he saw that the space beyond was a great shaft, striped with horizontal rings of light. Here, if anywhere, the geas would make itself felt again. He set down his bundle, opened his wallet, and drew out the wrapped parcel of figurine, sticks, gray powder. He set the figurine upright on the floor, in the glow of the ring. Around it he made a circle of crossed sticks, and inside the circle poured the gray powder.

He took tinder and shavings from his wallet, dropped them along the circle of sticks. He drew out his fire stick, loaded it with more tinder, drove the plunger home. A feeling of tension gathered inside him. He dropped the burning tinder on the pile, breathed it into flame, chanted, "Die, Goryat! Die, Goryat, die!"

The sticks kindled, the flame ran around the circle, the gray powder flared up with a whoosh. The figurine was obscured for a moment; when the smoke cleared, its face was blackened.

The tension was gone; there was an emptiness in its place. Thorinn hopped forward. Where the tunnel met the shaft, it flared out smoothly above and below; the floor dropped away with a deceptive gentleness, like water pouring over the lip of a chasm, and the light-rings became ovals instead of circles. To either side, the upright rings gave way to the horizontal rings of the shaft. He had only to descend to the lowest ring in the flared mouth of the tunnel, then step onto the nearest horizontal ring and begin to climb.

Thorinn hoisted his bundle to his shoulders again, climbed down the slope onto the first horizontal ring. The dark upper surface of the ring was flat and level, and two spans wide; he was able to hop upon it with ease, knowing that if he stumbled he could reach up to catch himself against the lighted surface of the ring. He was aware of the gulf beside him, but did not think of it. Above, the shaft was lighted for sixty ells, then vanished into darkness.

He began to climb: one hand on the curving undersurface of

the ledge above, a hop, the other hand on the top of the ledge; then both hands on top, pulling himself up; one knee over, a twist, and he was sitting on the ledge. Up to his feet, reaching for the ledge above, a hop, a twist, over and over. As he climbed, he thought of Goryat: had he really killed the old man? He was sure not. But what a shock it must have given him!

Pausing to rest, he glanced down into the great pit and thought he saw a movement, a flicker of wings. Now he was sure. The dark shape drifted nearer, growing as it came. Now he could see the cruel head tilted up, the yellow eyes staring. It was a great gray bird with pinions of polished metal. The beak opened, the great wings beat the air. Thorinn turned, drawing his sword, but all his movements were sluggish, benumbed. The bird was on him, blotting out the light; the wings buffeted his face. The ledge tilted away, gone; he was twisting in the air.

Go down, said the voice triumphantly.

6

How Thorinn fell five hundred leagues in a day and a night.

3215 A.D.

   . . . For these and other weighty reasons, as, to permit an equal and governable expansion of the matter at the centre of our globe, which, being confin'd, must else burst forth in earthquake and volcano whenas the burden above it shall be abated; to advantage ourselves of the aforesaid pressure and heat for the driving of our engines; as well as to increase fourfold the extent of our lands upon the surface by the removal of the oceans to the chamber below: it is our intention to drill three shafts to the centre of the Earth, taking matter for conversion from these shafts alone, until what time they shall be complete and the central chamber hollow'd out. The energy so obtain'd, by all our calculations, will satisfy our wants during the next twenty centuries. . . .

   Thorinn was falling. The lighted ledges flashed by as swift as eyeblinks, flick, flick, an ell out of reach. The wind of his passage had grown so strong that he could open his eyes only an instant before they filled with tears. As he turned, it whipped his back, his legs, then belly and face again. The sound of it filled his skull, like a gale sweeping across the bowl of Hovenskar. It had been steady, but now it began to buffet him, turning him this way and that, so that he spun now head down, now flat in the air like a falling leaf. The ledges of the great shaft around him blurred steadily upward.

The buffeting died away, and an instant later he felt a slight jar, as if he had passed through some flimsy barrier; then the buffeting came back. A short time later the same thing happened again, and, after an equal interval, still again. His mind took up the rhythm and he knew to the instant when the next check would come. After each one he felt a dull pain in his ears. His stomach knotted and he began to vomit. Long after his stomach was empty, he continued to retch feebly.

Time passed. The wind burned his face, and whipped his garments against his body until he was sore. Weariness overcame him. He had been falling for hours, and still there was no end. His eyes were streaming tears, the lids now so swollen that he could hardly open them. He held up one arm to shield his eyes; then, that failing, fumbled at the shoulder loops of his pack. He managed to slip one arm out, then the other. The wind fought him for the pack, but he pulled it around in front of his body, picked at it with numb fingers. When he had loosened the last knot, the wind instantly unrolled the cloth, scattering the contents, and turned it into a frantically flapping rag. He clutched it with knees and elbows; little by little he succeeded in drawing it tighter from head to crotch, and at last tied the ends together. The cloth shielded his face somewhat from the wind. At intervals, looking sideward, he could catch glimpses of the streaming wall of the shaft. Closer at hand, other things were falling. He recognized the talking box, and another box with its lid burst open and a cloud of little figurines around it. They were tumbling, shifting like midges; then they streamed upward and were gone, though the box continued to fall beside him.

Under the constant buffeting of the wind Thorinn grew dizzy and numb. His eyes closed more and more frequently. He roused once, with a start, to realize that he had been asleep. Nothing had changed. His eyes closed again, and presently he dreamed that he was falling down the long slope of the hillside in Hovenskar, under the half-dark, half-bright sky; the horses stood gazing in wonder as he drifted above the grass-tops toward the little hut which remained as distant as ever, no matter how long he fell.

Then his dreams grew confused, and he thought he was wandering under the earth, in a tunnel that opened from the bottom of the dry well in Hovenskar; he discovered a treasure house, and robbed it of jewels, and marvelous engines, and a magic box that spoke to him in a human voice; but the box spoke nonsense. Then he had fallen down the well again, and the well had no bottom, but went down endlessly into the center of the earth.

He awoke to the buffeting of the wind. His head ached, his eyes were gummy, his mouth dry. The cloth he had wrapped around him was flapping ceaselessly against his body: through its folds he could see the wall of the shaft spinning by. He knew he had been asleep a long time; yet he was still falling, and nothing had changed. Remembering his dream, he thought: what if there is no bottom?

He stretched and groaned. He was bruised in every limb, he needed to empty his bladder, and he felt both hunger and thirst. He found the water jug in his wallet and loosened the wrappings around it. While he waited for it to fill, he munched on a piece of cheese he found in the wallet; then he carefully took out the jug, put the spout to his lips and tried to drink. Water splashed over his mouth and nose, along with gemstones that pelted his face. Thorinn hastily covered the mouth of the jug with his palm, leaving only the spout free, and tried again. This time he was more successful; a trickle of water entered his mouth, ceased, then came again as he turned. His thirst was not satisfied, but he wrapped the jug again and put it away.

He dozed again and awoke, tormented by the aching of his head. The need to empty his bladder grew unbearable, and at last he pulled down his breeks and made shift to direct the stream out through the opening in his cover, where the wind dashed it into spray. He wrapped himself up and drifted off again into numb, uneasy sleep.

He awoke with a pang of alarm. Something had changed: the wind was like a great hand that smote him on the breast and back as he turned. The wall of the shaft was moving past him more slowly, still more slowly, flick, flick . . . flick . . . flick. . . . It slowed almost to a crawl; the wind belabored him. Past the fluttering edge of the cloth, he glimpsed a dark band between the rings of the shaft. It tipped nearer; he had only time to realize that he was falling toward it, and then the wind abruptly was gone, and he lay sprawled, dizzy and too numb to cry out his surprise, on a smooth floor that slipped away under him.

He clawed for purchase. Silence rang in his ears like a shout, and his skin tingled to the absence of the wind. The slope under him turned abruptly deeper; he was sliding, falling again. Now he did cry out, and struggled to right himself. The feeling of great space was gone; the air felt close. He struck something hard and was at rest in the heaving blackness. There was a tinkling somewhere below, then silence.

After several attempts, he managed to sit upright. He was in absolute darkness. The surface under him seemed to be composed of thin metal ribs that ran crosswise to each other, leaving square holes half a span wide between them. His fingers slipped down into these apertures, and touched nothing. The ribs were hard, but not uncomfortable to sit upon; a puzzle—they felt harder to his fingers than to his buttocks.

He listened intently, heard nothing. Balancing himself with care, he opened his wallet and got out his light-box. The moss glowed dimly in the lighted end. He carefully transferred a pinch of sky-moss from each compartment to the other. The lighted compartment went dark, and the dark one flared up brightly. He turned the box upward, saw a glimmering crosshatch of metal over his head. This was a floor like the one he sat on, but the ribs were much more widely spaced, leaving squares two ells across. Through one of these, evidently, he had fallen.

He turned the light-box downward, with caution because the lighted end was the one from which he had lost the mica. He thought he could make out a dark floor below, but did not dare turn the box straight downward.

A few ells away lay his sword, beside a square object which he recognized as the talking box. All the rest of his looted treasures had vanished; except for the cloth, box and sword, they had all been small enough to drop through the holes in the floor, and although he swept the beam of the light-box in every direction, he could not find them.

He opened his wallet, drew out the magic jug, unwrapped it, and set it down. Most of the jewels were still in it. While he waited for the jug to fill with water, he identified by touch the rest of the things in the wallet: his fire stick, some pebbles from Hovenskar, a strip of horse-meat, a half-empty box of cheese. He ate a little of the cheese, but his thirst was so great that he could not swallow much. He tipped the jug to his lips, drank the trickle of water that came out, set the jug down again.

He was dizzy, but he managed to crawl a few ells away, where he took down his breeks and relieved himself, squatting over one of the holes in the floor.

He crawled back to the talking box. It lay face up, and he could see a flicker of color in the dark crystal. "Box," he said.

"I am here."

"Box, tell me, what is this place?"

"This is a place where things fall."

Thorinn said, "Why?"

"Why do things fall?"

"Yes."

"All things fall to other things." The crystal lighted up, and he could see some sort of complicated shape moving across it. "I don't mean that," he said impatiently. "I mean, why here? What is this place for?"

The crystal went dark. "This place is to take things that fall here. This place not, then things fall to the bottom, on heads of people."

Thorinn considered this. "Are there people at the bottom?"

"Yes."

"How far is it to the bottom?"

"It is two hundred hundreds of hundreds and sixty hundreds of hundreds of ells."

Thorinn frowned. "You mean thousands?" he ventured.

"What is a thousand?"

"A thousand is ten hundreds."

"It is two thousands of thousands and six hundreds of thousands of ells."

Thorinn tried to imagine such a number, and gave it up. "Well then, how far is it to the top again?"

"It is four thousands of thousands and four hundreds of thousands of ells."

Thorinn put his head in his hands. He remembered the fall, the wind buffeting him, such a wind as he had never felt even riding Stonebreaker into the teeth of a gale in Hovenskar. He must have

been falling ten times as fast as a horse could gallop, at least . . .
and it had gone on for hours. He remembered the rings of the
shaft wall whipping by him till they blurred together. He thought
of that going on hour after hour, while he slept, still falling. . . .

"Box, are there people living near here?"

"Yes."

"Which is the best way to get to them?"

"Engines will come to take things from this place. Engines will
take you to the people."

Thorinn disliked the sound of this. "Show me these engines," he
said.

Colors began to appear in the crystal. "Wait a minute,"
Thorinn said, and hitched himself across the ribbed floor until he
could reach the box and turn it upright. The crystal had gone
dark. He moved back a little, to see better. "All right."

In the crystal, two spiderlike things of metal appeared. They
had metal eyes and waving metal arms with claws at the end, and
they moved in a way that made Thorinn ill to watch.

"That's enough," he said hastily. "Box, I don't want to wait for
the engines—how can I get out of here by myself?"

"At the back of this place there are—" The crystal lighted; it
showed a wall of metal with three panels that opened and shut as
he watched.

"Doors?"

"Yes, doors."

"All right, then." Thorinn leaned over far enough to reach the
piece of stuff, pulled it to him, and wrapped the box in it. The
strips he had tied it with earlier were gone; he cut new ones off the
end of the cloth to make shoulder loops, as before, and slung the
pack on his back. There was still something disturbing and odd
about all his movements; his arms seemed unnaturally light, and
when he moved them they went farther than he meant them to. It
was like what had happened when Snorri's Pipe began to roar;
then all things had lost somewhat of their weight, but this was
much worse. Leaning forward cautiously and pressing with one
hand on the floor, he straightened his legs and managed to stand
up. The floor above was an ell or so over his head. Shining the
light between the ribs, he saw a dim reflected gleam from the ceiling, then another, nearer, from a wall that sloped gently up into

darkness. It seemed that he was in a kind of midden-hole, into which things fell and sorted themselves out by their sizes.

His first step took him high in the air; he clutched at the nearest rib of the floor above, overbalanced, and drifted down kicking helplessly to land on his back. He sat astonished, then got up and tried again. This time, using only his toes, he was able to keep his balance, though he floated as high as an ordinary stride would have taken him. He tried again, with still better results. He turned and began to follow the dancing beam of the light-box. After a stride or two he realized that the floor sloped gently downward toward the rear of the chamber; probably that accounted for part of his trouble in learning to stand up and walk. Ahead, something gleamed out of the darkness: it was an upright surface, formed of metal ribs set crosswise to each other like the floor he walked on. Beyond it the floor continued, but now it was solid metal.

Approaching the barrier, he discovered that it was made in sections that stood close together; each section was about four ells wide. There was no door to be seen, although he turned left and followed the barrier until it met the wall of the chamber, then right to the opposite wall.

As he turned back to the middle again, his eye was caught by a spark of red fire below; then two more, of a greenish hue, a little distance away. He turned his light beam on them as well as he could through the ribs of the floor, and thought they were his lost jewels, but could not be sure; nor could he see any means of getting them.

He turned to the barrier and this time examined the nearest section, to see how it was made fast to the floor. He found it was held only by three metal contrivances that curved over the bottom rib and were fixed to the floor on the other side. Putting his hand between the ribs, he fumbled at one of these, and finding a handle pressed it, whereupon the contrivance sprang back and released the rib. He did the same with the other two, and now felt the barrier loose in his hands at the bottom, though it was still fixed at the top. He pressed against it, and it swung up easily.

Crouching there with one hand holding the barrier over his head, he swung the light-beam back and forth over the floor. The floor ended a few ells in front of him; beyond was blackness. The feel of the air on his face, the timbre of the few sounds he made, spoke of a vast empty space.

He let the barrier down softly and fell to examining the floor around him. It was really a sort of platform, and above him there was another, of the same dull brownish metal, which seemed to extend farther out than this one. There was a light coating of dust on the floor; under it he could see scuff-marks, as if something had been dragged toward the edge of the platform. He thought of the spidery engines the box had shown him. By the look of the floor, he thought the engines had not been here in a long time; but perhaps they only came when something fell into the chamber.

He held his breath and listened, staring at the blackness that filled the space between the platform he stood on and the one above. He began to be uneasy about his light, and capped the end of the box, but that was worse: now the blackness swelled forward to touch his face.

With the light-box uncapped again, but shielding it with his fingers, he followed the barrier until he reached the wall. This was of solid brownish metal, not a grillwork like the others, but there was a door in it. It was not quite like the doors the box had shown him. He fumbled with the handle until he discovered how it worked, and slid the door open. Inside was more blackness, in which his light-beam picked out a few ambiguous shapes, a wall, a ceiling.

He closed the door. He was in a room, about the size of the platform outside. The ceiling was broken; dust and rubble covered the floor. He examined some of the metal devices that stood here and there, but could make nothing of them. One or two were like melted chairs; they would be ill to sit in, and he could imagine no other use for them.

The damage was worst at the far end of the chamber. Here the walls were blackened, and a great hole gaped in the ceiling; tongues of corroded metal hung down; broken stones were piled high in the corner. A faint breath came from the opening above. Thorinn climbed the slope, peered upward past the beam of his light. The way was partially blocked at the opening by fallen slabs of stone; beyond, it seemed to be clear. He tested the slabs cautiously, then began to wriggle past them.

The passage widened perceptibly as he went on, until he was able to crawl on hands and knees. It sloped gradually upward, twisting and turning. After a hundred ells or so it turned sharply to the right and forked into two ascending passages, both deep but narrow. The breath of air from the right-hand passage seemed a little stronger than the other, and he chose that one. For a while the passage was deep enough to let him scramble half-erect; then it twisted again and began to grow shallower. In another ell or two he found himself in difficulty. The passage had grown so narrow that he could not get through it with the bundle on his shoulders. He retreated until he could crouch far enough to work the pack free. Pushing it ahead of him, he was able to advance another ten ells, the passage growing steadily narrower as he went. Then the passage took an abrupt downward turn. He thrust the pack down ahead of him, wriggled after it. It checked, then jammed tight. He tugged to free it, and it came back a finger's-breadth or two, then held fast again; it felt as if some loop or projecting fold of the stuff had caught.

He probed with his fingers at the end of the bundle, all around. At one point he felt a faint touch of cool air. He squirmed forward, forcing his arm between the bundle and the smooth stone. Halfway down, he felt the bulge of the talking box inside. He got a precarious grip and tugged. Sweat ran into his eyes. He tugged with one hand, pushed with the other. The bundle turned slightly. He braced himself and pushed hard. The bundle ground forward, stopped, moved again, and suddenly dropped out of reach. A freshet of cool air played against his face. The light-box, sliding down after the pack, dropped and disappeared. He heard it fall, and saw its beam not far below.

A squirm and a heave, and he was out, falling, twisting slowly to land without a sound.

He sat up, bruised and gasping. He was in a level passage, blocked at one end by a fall of stones; in the other direction, it ran off straight into darkness. He had gone no more than a hundred ells when he saw the circular opening of a shaft in the ceiling. He bent his knee slightly, leaped into the shaft, twisting to brace himself with foot and elbow.

As he had thought, the shaft was closed by a shield of brown metal, but there was no opening in it and it would not turn. He pushed against it and thought he felt it give a little. He braced himself more firmly, pushed again. The shield gave way, as if hinged at one side. Dim light washed down into the shaft, and he smelled fresh air. He lunged upward, pulled himself through, and sprawled in a tangle of stiff brown canes. The shield clapped shut behind him. Leaf shadows trembled on his face, and he smelled the scent of green trees.

7

How Thorinn was the guest of demons, and how he repaid their hospitality.

In the year of the Broken Branches an untested warrior of the clan of Blue Snake pushed his sister into a thorn tree and wounded her grievously, whereon she cursed him, saying, "May the sky demons come for you!" The young warrior unluckily replied, "This for you, and the sky demons as well!"

A year and a day after, two sky demons entered the lodge of Blue Snake in the guise of a bareskinned person and a talking gourd. They were bound and tormented by Blue Snake and other persons of his lodge, but escaped by magic arts and slew many before they returned to the sky. Afterward the clan of Blue Snake, being weakened by these slayings, fell easy prey to the clan of Break Skulls, who took the women captive, slew and ate the others after tormenting them for five nights and days. Thus the lodge of Blue Snake fell vacant, and being an unlucky place, was not tenanted again save by moths and deathbeetles.

He found himself in a thicket of tall canes with leafy tops, which crossed over his head and shut out the sky. A bird was sing-

ing somewhere not far away. Sprawled among the canes, Thorinn
listened with such pleasure that for moments he forgot what he
was about.

When he turned to look at the shield, he found in its place a
gray rounded boulder, half buried in the earth. Thorinn knelt to
examine this, pushed against it, but it would not move. He began
to feel dizzy again, and thought of lying down to sleep, but there
was no room for that here, between the canes and the boulder.

He got up and began to climb, finding himself so light that he
could ascend to the very tip of a cane. As he emerged from the
thicket, clinging to the leafy top with only his head protruding
from it, he was looking into a remote tangle of curved milky
stems, as if he had somehow got into the roots of the canes instead
of their tops. The illusion was so strong that he was dizzy once
more and had to shut his eyes a moment. When he opened them it
was no better, until he looked down along the dwindling stem of
the cane. All around him at a lower level were the flat green tops
of other canes, and by keeping them in view he was able to per-
suade himself that the world was the right way up. He saw now
that the canes, tall as they had seemed before, were like grasses at
the feet of those immense tangled growths whose shapes he could
not quite make out. The sky was invisible, somewhere far above.
Once he thought he saw a flicker of motion deep in the tangle of
stems, but it did not come again. The air was still and cool.

While he hung there, a silent gloom rushed over the landscape.
One moment the world was full of color; next, the light dwindled
and went out behind him. In the blackness, Thorinn clung without
up or down, or any direction to guide him. Shortly, however, his
eyes began to grow accustomed to the darkness, and he could
make out the same enigmatic tangled growths as before; but all
were transformed in the green skylight that filtered through the
branches. A cool air had sprung up. Somewhere in the distance insects began to shrill; and there were other sounds.

In the tangle that spread wide around him, some of the wavering branches and stems were the color of cheese, some black as
beetles; the hollows between them were purple, crow's-wing blue,
deepest green. Thorinn heard a slithering movement not far away;
then wings hummed past his head, and he ducked. He tried to
slide back down the stem, but at first moved so slowly that he felt
almost as if he were going the wrong way, up into the sky. He

relaxed the grip of his legs, but still moved with uncanny slowness, and in the end he had to propel himself downward hand under hand.

When he was beneath the shelter of the cane tops, he came to a halt. Now that he was quiet, he could hear faint, enigmatic sounds from below: rustlings, clicks. They made him uneasy, and he began to wish that he had been quieter a moment ago. He slid down, silent except for the whisper of his hands on the stem. Now he was near enough to touch the next cane. He leaned out, grasped it, and swung over. The cane dipped slowly, grating against another; he transferred to that, and then had to kick away to prevent the cane he had just left from wiping him off again. He stopped to listen. The sounds below were nearer: click; rustle; scrape.

The stem he lay on began to vibrate. Thorinn stared into the shadows. Something was crawling up the stem: he saw the green dots of its eyes. The cane shivered again. The thing was coming closer with surprising speed; now he could make out that it had a thick dark body, a confusion of moving knobby legs like a cricket's. Thorinn rolled over and began to stand up, meaning to see if he could shake the stalk until the thing fell off; but he had forgotten how slowly things moved here, and while his feet were still drifting in a leisurely way back toward the cane, the insect-thing was suddenly in front of his nose. It had sharp mouth-parts that gleamed as they opened wide. His back stiffened, he kicked out, and hung in midair while the cane swayed above him. He saw the dark thing leap, felt it strike his legs like a sack of meal, then a stabbing pain as its jaws gripped him through the leather. He had the sword out, swung and struck—another pain, he had gashed his own leg, and the insect-thing, cut in two, went spinning away. Now the cane was drifting toward him, a little to one side. It dipped, touched him, he trying awkwardly to turn and seize it, but he went off again, thrashing his arms. Now the spinning world steadied; it was moving past his feet; the dark meadow came nearer, he bent his knees and staggered, but only with surprise: the shock of landing was no more than that of stepping off a waist-high stone.

His good leg began to hurt. He put his fingers to it, found a gash in the leather and a little blood. He straightened, shifting hands on the sword again. Something moved past him. There was a thump in the grass not far away, then another, nearer. Thorinn did not stop to think; he leaped.

As he went up, something small and swift passed under him. Next moment he felt a sharp blow on his good foot, a scrabbling of claws on the leather. Whatever it was, the thing slipped off and he saw it fall toward the dark grass. The tree was turning majestically around him. He twisted and revolved his arms, trying to straighten himself out, and partially succeeded. There was a sizzling noise at his ear, then something stung him on the neck. He slapped at it, and found himself gyrating again. A misshapen loop of vine came by; he grasped it, swung helplessly a moment, then pulled himself up into the tree.

He stood aslant on a tree-limb or old vine, breathless, looking down at the grass an incredible distance below—twenty ells, at least, perhaps more; it was hard to tell in the greenlight. He felt exultant; if he could jump like that, no matter what was after him. . . .

Down there in the dimlit grass, something moved. It was round and gray, and it was hanging in the air—no, rising toward him— larger, a tangle of knobby limbs— With a startled cry, Thorinn leaped backward and upward. Something dealt him a heavy blow across the back; then leaves were whipping his face. Another blow; he clutched a limb and swung to rest. The leaves below him continued to rustle. There was a thrashing, then a measured grating and crunching sound, as if something brittle and hard were being eaten.

Thorinn retreated, pulling himself upward by degrees. A creeper on which he put his hand turned supple, bent toward him, and became a long legless creature with a flickering tongue. Thorinn flung it away, and climbed still more carefully, keeping to open spaces as well as he could. He was beginning to sweat. Nearby something swayed under a massive limb. It looked like a shaggy fruit, but it was big enough to hold five men. Thorinn avoided it and climbed. A little higher, two limbs growing level and side by side had put out branches to each other, making a platform ten ells long from which, here and there, other trees grew. At the end of this platform was something that looked remarkably like a hut.

Thorinn approached the platform, found it had a floor of canes interwoven with the branches. The place was silent and empty.

The hut at the far end had a peaked roof and an open doorway; it was half-walled, with black space showing all around under the roof.

Thorinn's weariness took him: he went quietly up to the doorway and looked in. The hut was empty except for some mats in one corner. When he had made sure of this, Thorinn stood still and listened. The tree was full of faint movements, but none seemed near or threatening. He sat down on the mats, removed his pack and leaned against the wall, sword in hand. After a time he caught himself dozing and sat up with a start. The night was still. He closed his eyes, merely to rest them.

He came awake with his heart pounding, knowing that he must not move. Outside in the greenlight, something gray and misshapen drifted down and disappeared beyond the half-wall of the hut; Thorinn felt the faint thump when it landed. It was like a man, but there was something wrong with it. He glimpsed another one falling, then heard low, grunting voices. He reached for his pack and put his arms through the loops, trying not to make a sound, but by ill luck the corner of the pack scraped against the floor. Instantly a gray form was in the doorway, another peering over the wall. Thorinn turned, dived over the opposite wall into the darkness. Something caught his leg as he went over, bringing him down hard against the platform, and he struck his head a blow that made it ring. When he tried to get up, he found his leg still held fast. The platform rustled and shook all around him. He glimpsed another gray shape and smelled its rank odor; then something struck him a harder blow on the cheekbone, and he drifted away into blackness.

When he came to himself, he could not at first remember what had happened. He was hanging in midair while a rough gray wall moved by jerks past his face. He was uncomfortable, and tried to move his limbs to ease them, but could not. His face hurt; one eye would not open. Jerk; up he went again. His arms were behind him, bent over a stick that came out under his armpit on either side, and his wrists were tied to his ankles. Voices were muttering somewhere overhead. Jerk; a dark leafy twig passed, and the gray wall became a tree-trunk, lumpy, scarred, fissured, and immense. It swung around, this way and that. Thorinn craned his head back. He saw now that a cord, attached to him somewhere behind, rose over the edge of a giant limb just above. A gray face with lumi-

nous green eyes peered down at him briefly, and was gone. Up he
went again, swinging. The stick that protruded under his arm
touched the tree-trunk and caught; he revolved slowly until his
body was pointing out away from the tree. More voices. He rose
another span and stopped; now the stick was caught under the
limb. After a moment something gray and supple came over the
edge of the limb and dropped toward him. He had barely time to
flinch before the thing was on his back. Its legs clasped him
around the hips; its arms appeared over his shoulders and pushed
him away from the tree. The arms were gray and hairy; the hands
were like a man's. Thorinn fell into despair, for now he knew he
had been captured by demons.

He revolved again as the demon freed one end of the stick. The
other end was still caught, and he swung slowly around that, then
the demon freed it in turn, and he rose, swinging inward until his
head struck the limb and he checked again. Then the demon
leaped off his back, and in a moment he began to rise, scraping his
face and chest against the wrinkled bark. Two of the creatures
stood above, pulling on the cord, and others hung from the openings in the tangle nearby. They were smaller than men, their arms
grotesquely long, legs short. When they had brought him within
reach, two demons seized him and pulled him up level with them;
the cord, meanwhile, had disappeared into a dark hole above, and
they thrust him up headfirst into it. The cord tightened, he rose,
and a dark passage swallowed him. He swung as he went up, first
this way, then that. The wall of the passage, when he bumped it
with his head or feet, seemed dry and yielding. After a time a faint
glow appeared; it was less than the nightlight outside, but he could
see the two demons who pulled him up out of the passage, and beyond them a deep chamber.

The demons lifted him and propped him carelessly against a
wall. His head and feet touched the wall, but his knees hung clear
of the floor, and he realized that besides the stick under his arms,
there was another set crosswise to it. It occurred to him for the
first time that his pack was gone, and the box with it; whether his
wallet and sword were there he could not tell.

Such light as there was came from dimly luminous patches on
walls and floor, as if sky-moss had been rubbed there. In the
gloom, the demons came and went. The chamber was immensely
tall; although his open eye was uppermost, Thorinn could not see

the top. The demons went up and down with great swiftness, using
cords that hung from the upper part of the chamber and poles that
stood across it. In going up, they sometimes leaped from one pole
to the next, but most often climbed the cords, so lightly that they
hardly seemed to touch. In coming down, they used the poles,
leaping head downward from one to another until they reached
the last, when they swung around and dropped to the floor. None
came near Thorinn.

He tried to break or loosen the cords around his wrists, without success. Then he thought that if he could work his way upward along the one stick, the other stick, being attached to the
first, would move downward along his back, and he might get
some freedom for his arms. But although he was able to grip the
stick between his thighs, he could not move his legs enough to accomplish anything.

After a time there was a stir above, and a swarm of demons
dropped into view. Three of these were females, as large as
Thorinn, a head or more taller than the other demons, and he realized dimly that the others must be their young. The females
crowded close around him, muttering and grunting; they took
turns fingering his garments, tugging at his belt, prodding him.
Their eyes were big and green. Two or three of the small demons
dived down the hole in the floor, followed after a moment by the
rest. Two of the big females turned, sprang up, and were lost to
view in the gloom; the third went across the chamber and, hanging
by one hand from some protuberance, took something out of a
sack there and began to eat it.

The strain on Thorinn's shoulders and hips grew painful. He
tried to ease it by flexing his body, but his legs were drawn back
so tightly that he could hardly move. The female demon finished
whatever she was eating and took another piece. Thorinn found
that he could push outward with his feet against the wall; it meant
pulling his arms even tighter against the stick, but anything was
better than lying still, and he did it again and again, rocking farther out each time, until he overbalanced and fell on his face. Now
he was entirely helpless; the most he could do was rock from side
to side a little. The muscles of his legs and buttocks began to
cramp.

After a long time the demon came back and lifted him by the
stick, propping him against the wall again. She had something

round in her hand; she took a bite of it, and bright juice ran down
her chin. She held the thing out; its pungent smell made Thorinn
swallow. He opened his dry mouth. Quickly, with her other hand,
she thrust a wad of dirt and trash into his mouth. Thorinn spat it
out—dry leaves, filth—and spat, and spat. Across the room the
demon was grunting in a slow rhythm, and he realized at length
that the creature was laughing.

More time passed. The demon left off eating and picked up a
half-finished mat from the floor. She began working at it, holding
it with her feet while she braided the long strips together. Thorinn
remembered the sound of the river purling down endlessly against
the stones, dropping away, spurting, trickling, falling in sheets
below. Cool and clean, clean and cool. He saw the demon put her
work away and get up. The wall shook, then small demons were
erupting into the room, dozens of them, followed after a moment
by bigger ones—bigger even than the females. The room was full
of them, they were hanging from the walls and the climbing poles.
They were all around him, they jerked him away from the wall
and stood him up on his stick, crowding close, turning him this
way and that, rumbling and grunting to each other. They were a
head taller than Thorinn, wider but thinner than the females.
Their spindly arms were stronger than they looked. One of them
tugged impatiently at Thorinn's belt, then fumbled with the buckle
until he got it open and dragged off the belt, which another imme-
diately snatched away from him. A third pulled down Thorinn's
breeks; a fourth yanked his head back, pulled his jaw open and
stared into his mouth. The uproar was stunning; all the males
grunting at once, the children and females leaping back and forth
overhead, and Thorinn shoved this way and that until his head
spun.

He felt a sharp tug at his wrists, then a slackening. His legs
were released, and a moment later one of the males was pulling
off his breeks and holding them up for the others to see.

Thorinn's feet trailed on the floor like dead things; it was only
the stick and the demons' hands that held him upright. After a moment he felt someone working at his wrists too; then they were
released, the crossed sticks pulled away and he began to fall. But
the demons hauled him upright again and tugged his shirt off over
his head. Someone held him up by his hair while the rest examined
him minutely, feeling his skin, pressing muscles, poking fingers

into ribs. Thorinn could not prevent this; he could move his arms a little, but not his legs, and his hands felt like lumps of meat. At some point they had got his shoes off, too, and were passing them around. Thorinn saw one huge male holding up the belt and pointing to it, his mouth opening and closing. In the general din he could not hear anything, but others could; they crowded toward the demon with the belt, then dispersed again, and the commotion spread. A knot of struggling figures formed halfway up the wall, broke and dropped to the floor. Other demons crowded in, wedging Thorinn tighter, but those approaching from the rear forced their way through. In the midst of these were two demon children, gripped by their hair and squalling. One of the old demons barked at them, pointing to Thorinn and then to the belt which he shook in their faces. Thorinn could see that he was pointing first to one place on the belt and then another, and guessed that they were the worn places where his wallet and sword had hung. The children answered; the old demon cuffed them. The children disappeared into the crowd, followed by some of the adults.

Thorinn's arms and legs now felt as if a thousand needles were in them. Heedless of the pain, he began trying to open and close his fingers. The crowd was thinning a little; sounds of scuffling broke out on the other side of the chamber. Thorinn saw demon children dancing up the walls with gobbets of meat in their hands. A few adults followed, and squatted on the poles munching. Now Thorinn could see that the women were cutting up the carcass of some large animal; it must have been fresh-killed, for he could see the flesh steaming.

The demon who was holding Thorinn suddenly turned him about and brought his arms together behind his back. Thorinn tried to resist, but was still too weak; the demon wrapped a cord around his wrists and knotted it. Then, holding Thorinn propped casually in one elbow, he unfastened another cord from around his waist and made a loop in the end. He dropped the loop over Thorinn's head, tightened it a little, then flung the other end of the cord to a demon who sat overhead. Thorinn felt the cord tighten under his chin, then he was rising. He stopped, hung swaying; he tried vainly to touch the floor with his good foot. The noose was too stiff for his weight alone to tighten it as long as he hung still, but at the slightest movement it crept inward across the underside of his jaw. Rather than be throttled, he held himself motionless and kept his head back.

A demon, crossing the room on his way back to the carcass, casually wiped his hand on Thorinn's body. The push set him swinging; the room lurched around him. A demon child threw down a squalid lump of something that splattered on his ribs. In a moment another missile took him on the ear, and then he was being bombarded from every side. Each blow altered the direction of his swing and made him rotate more erratically. A demon came from the shadows carrying a long stick. He poked it at Thorinn's side; the pain made him writhe in spite of himself, and the movement tightened the noose. Another demon with a stick came forward from the opposite side. Facing each other, without excitement, the two began jabbing Thorinn by turns as he swung. The sticks pierced him in the chest, the side, the buttocks, the chest again.

After a time the thrusts stopped. Thorinn opened his good eye and saw that there had been an interruption: a crowd had formed again around the old demons who sat against the wall nearby. He saw two children leaping away, then the glint of metal. It was his sword; the demons were passing it from hand to hand, and his wallet too, and now he saw a square shape that could only be his talking box.

He was not sure whether he could speak. He uttered a croak, then tried again: "Box!"

"I am here."

Relief almost unmanned him. He said, "Box, tell them to untie my hands." Demons were leaning over in surprised attitudes, peering at the box. There was a flicker of color in the crystal, almost too faint to see. Now demons came leaping across the room, falling from the shadows above. The two demons with the sticks had gone with the rest. In the uproar, Thorinn cried again to the box, but could not tell if it had heard.

After a time the crowd began to disperse. Thorinn saw an old demon holding the box, and two other old ones beside him. The din of voices had died away a little, and Thorinn called, "Box, did you tell them?"

"I told them."

The two demons with the sticks were back, and now one of the old ones came forward carrying the sword. He stopped and thrust the sword several times toward Thorinn's belly without touching him, all the while carrying on a grunted exchange with the other two demons. "Box, what are they saying?" Thorinn asked.

"I do not know what they are saying."

"Then how did you talk to them?"

"I talked to them in pictures."

Thorinn went cold. "What else did you tell them?"

"They asked about the sword, and I showed them it was better than a stick for cutting."

The old one with the sword stepped back; the two with sticks ranged themselves on either side of Thorinn. A fourth demon came up behind; Thorinn felt its hands on the cord around his wrists, and his heart grew big.

The cord fell away. Thorinn reached for the noose; one of the stickmen promptly leaned forward and pierced his hand. The shock was so great that Thorinn lost his wits and reached with his other hand for the noose. The stickman on the other side pierced that hand also.

The demons had gathered in a ring. The old one with the sword exchanged several remarks with the stickmen; then, apparently satisfied, he stepped forward, put the tip of the sword against Thorinn's belly and cut downward. Blood began to crawl down Thorinn's leg. In spite of himself, his hand jerked toward the noose, and again the stickman pierced it. "Box," he cried.

"Here am I."

The old demon stepped up, raising the sword. Thorinn's body writhed forward in desperation; the noose closed hard on his neck, but he seized the demon's wrist. A blow took him in the side. He kicked the demon's dim face, and the sword was in his hand. Another blow spun him around. He cut at the stickmen, making them leap back; strangling, he seized the cord above his head. The demon on the pole stood and reached for him as he flew up, the cord slackening. Air rattled into his throat. He raised the sword and smote through the demon's leg and the knotted cord and half the pole, still rising, and touched the pole to push himself still higher, the demon toppling now below him and screaming as it slowly fell in a cloud of blood (the world an uproar of grunting voices, fangs in open mouths, green eyes), and now he was at the next pole, a demon reaching for him, and he smote off its arm; then clutching the pole he climbed up and feeling the wall springy and fibrous under his hand he struck and opened a long gash, the cool night air entering, and dived through and was outside. He caught a curving branch, swung back, and glimpsed the chamber he had left as a dark sack bulging between two limbs. In his mind was a picture: Thorinn drops dwindling through the branches, the demons pursue, swarm around him, and their sticks pierce his body, limbs, face . . . No. He sprang for the demons' house again, clung to the fibrous wall just above the opening he had made, and waited, trembling with fear and hate.

When the first gray head emerged, he struck it with the hilt of his sword. The head dropped, the body followed it and with a thrust of his foot Thorinn helped it downward. He dealt with the second in the same way, then groped for a better handhold and sprang upward, wedging himself between wall and limb. There was a crashing of leaves far below just as the next pair of demons emerged; they dived for it unhesitatingly and were gone. Three more followed them, then two, then many; the wall trembled as they surged out, diving in their turn. Their voices called back and forth, far below.

When the tree was still except for the rattle and click of small things in the branches, Thorinn dropped to the opening again, slipped through and stood upon the pole inside. The chamber was empty except for two females who stared at him, then climbed the opposite wall with grunts of alarm. His clothing and possessions lay strewn on the floor. Thorinn descended, picked up the wallet first and put his hand in to make sure of the magic jug, light-box, and fire stick. His shoes and the cloth he had wrapped the box in were nowhere to be seen. He pulled on his shirt and breeks hastily, looped the wallet over his belt and buckled it on, thrust the sword through the belt—the scabbard was gone—then pulled out the light-box and uncapped it. Across the chamber, there were shrieks and scrambling sounds. He turned the light that way: out of their dark mystery, the walls of the chamber sprang up brown and ordinary; he glimpsed the females clinging to each other on a high pole; then he lowered the light beam, played it across the floor, saw his shoes at once and put them on. He could not find the cloth or scabbard, although he looked into some woven baskets and turned over half a dozen of the mats that covered the floor. The carcass of the half-slaughtered animal lay on the far

side of the chamber; it was smaller than he had thought and had a
blunt muzzle.

From a peg on the wall hung some cords of the kind that had
been used to tie him. He took one and looped it over his shoulder.
High above, the light-beam showed a platform. He leaped for it,
found it empty except for baskets and mats. Above it was another,
and here he found a mass of demon bodies huddled together along
the wall, all females, some with children clinging to them. One of
the children was holding something long and brown; Thorinn
leaned closer, saw that it was his missing scabbard. He eased it out
from between the demon child's fingers, little by little. When he
plucked it away at last, the child sighed and turned over, but did
not waken.

Thorinn leaped again, and at last came to the top of the chamber, where a row of wrapped bundles hung from a crosspole.
Clinging to this, he cut a slit in the brown dome overhead. He
capped the light-box and put it away, then thrust himself out into
the breathing night again. Around him the topmost branches of
the tree lifted themselves against a sky that seemed almost close
enough to touch.

Thorinn leaped to the nearest branch and began to climb. As he
drifted upward, he could see that the topmost branches did indeed
touch the sky, and some disappeared into it. Now the pure green
was close overhead; squinting against it, he put up a hand and felt
the moss cool and moist. He pulled off handfuls and stuffed them
into his wallet. In the hole he had made he felt a matted fibrous
substance like coarse-woven straw. He could force his fingers
through it, but when he tried to pull a hank of it free, it resisted; it
was all tangled together like the stalks of last season's grass.

The branch trembled. He looked down and saw gray shapes
leaping toward him; more were erupting from the dome below. He
rose almost without thinking, gripped the sky with one hand, and
swung himself out. He probed through the moss for another grip,
swung again. A thrown stick went past him, struck the sky and
spun silently into the void. He looked back. The demons had clustered at the end of a branch, which bending under their weight had
left them ells short of the sky. Another stick slid into the moss
with a tearing sound. Feeling light-headed, Thorinn plucked it out
and threw it back.

From a little distance, he looked back again. The demons were still clustered on the branch. He moved farther away, having an impulse to get clear of the tree: but could he survive a drop to the ground? While he hesitated, looking about him, he noticed a dark line in the sky not far ahead. He set out toward it; as he approached, the line expanded slowly to a narrow oval. When he was almost there, he turned and looked back again. Two demons were hanging under the sky, and as he watched, another leaped up. They came swinging toward him, and now he could see their eyes glinting under the green sky.

He tried to move faster; his fingers slipped and he almost fell. In his mind, the sky blazed. His breath caught; he gaped with excitement. Here was the opening, a hole in the sky three spans wide. Hanging beside it, Thorinn plunged his free hand into his wallet, found the light-box and pushed the cap off with his thumb, made sure that it was the broken end, the lighted one. He drew it out and aimed the light-beam into the faces of the demons, saw their eyes clench and their bellies contract. Then he jammed the open end of the box into the sky. Brightness exploded around him. Blinking, dazzled, he looked down and saw the treetops green in daylight; a hurrying shadow flickered at the edge of vision and was gone. Shrieks echoed below the treetops. The demons hung from the sky, unable to move.

Thorinn turned. The shaft was beside him, with a disk of brown metal at the top. He reached up, felt the shield rotate under his fingers. The opening came into view, an eye of darkness expanding until it filled the circle. Thorinn leaped up, blood drumming in his ears. He had just strength enough to pull himself through and roll aside in the darkness. The floor was as soft as goose down. He slept, and woke to drink from the magic jug, and slept again.

He woke, feverish, and plastered sky-moss over his wounds with hands that could barely hold it. He heard himself raving, and woke again listening for a voice that had just fallen silent. He fumbled for the light-box in his wallet. His hands were weak and sore, but he got the light-box out and managed to transfer a bit of moss from each compartment to the other.

He woke again knowing that he would live, and that he had passed into manhood by giving and receiving blows in battle.

There were two deep wounds in the back of his left hand, passing between the tendons and coming out at the palm. They were closed now, but the skin around them was angry for a finger's breadth. The wound in his other hand was shallower but more painful, a ragged tear slanting upward through the meat of his palm. There were puncture wounds in his chest, back, sides, and buttocks. The wound in his belly had closed; the skin all around it was red and hot to the touch. His eye was still swollen, but now he could see with it, and this, except for the nick on his leg that he had done himself, was all the tale of his wounds.

In time to come he would be proud of these scars, but he would always know that he had been sick with fear when he got them.

He was weak and very hungry. He ate some cheese from his wallet and drank more water, and presently vomited it up again, and slept. When he woke, still weaker, he ate again and this time kept the food down.

As time passed, he grew to dislike the sweet stench of his sickness. He undressed and bathed himself as well as he could, in the water from the jug, and felt a little better. He got up and explored the passage for a dozen ells in either direction, coming back to open the shield and drop his ordures into the dark world below. *Go down,* said the voice, but he was too weak to obey, and when he closed the shield again, the voice stopped. When he woke again, he walked a little farther, and the next time still farther, until he came to the end of the passage where it curved upward and became a steep ascending shaft, from which a faint current of air breathed in his face. He went back, ate, and slept again. When he got up, groaning with stiffness, he followed the shaft upward until after some thirty ells it broke into a larger tunnel. Lights came on in vast swooping arcs over his head as he rose, and the silent display was so gigantic that he nearly ducked in terror as he had done before.

He went back to the passage below, ate the last of his cheese, slept, and woke again. He was very hungry. He opened the shield; it was daylight below. *Go down.* And he must, to get food. He thought of leaving some mark in the sky so that he could find the place again; he reached for the thong that should have been around his calf, but it was not there, and he remembered that he had left them both in the demons' house. He took up the cord instead, and made a heavy knot in one end.

Holding the cord, he opened the shield and dropped through. As he fell, the shield turned; he supported himself for a moment by his fingertips on the edge just before it closed, and pulled down all but the knotted end of the cord. As he let go, the shield closed on the cord, and Thorinn hung from it, then reached around and took a grip in the sky. He swung out and hung for a moment breathing and blinking in the glare. He saw the tree in the distance with its crown of branches and the dark bulge of the demons' house between them. He was suddenly certain he could not get that far. He swung toward it in trembling haste until he was well over the tree, then let go and dropped.

The branches came up under him like a bed, and he was content to sprawl there, eyes closed, until his breathing was better. The tree below and around him was a tangle of limbs and branches, creepers, vines, and other plants growing all anyhow. He dropped to the next level where there were some red berries on a vine, but they were so bitter that one taste was enough. A little way below, he found a shaggy dark fruit like the one he had seen before, but not half so big; it was less than two ells long. He found a convenient perch and stabbed into it. Under the dry leafy shell was a skin of the thickness of two fingers, and under this a pulpy greenish-brown fruit. Having split the rind as far down as he could reach, Thorinn carved out a segment of the fruit and sampled it; it was at once sweet and tart, and made him avid for more. His hands were trembling. He cut out another section and ate that, and another, until his hunger was gone. Then he cut a larger piece, wrapped it well in leaves and put it in his wallet; and still what he left behind was enough to have fed a hundred men.

He climbed to the top of the branch and saw his way past the crown of the tree and the demons' house to the cord that hung from the sky. As he neared the house, he thought of the bundles hanging under the roof-tree, and was minded to go in and take a few, for they might be food, and he had nothing with him to eat but the fruit he had cut below. He leaped up onto the brown dome, but when he felt for the cut he had made before, he found it had been sealed up from inside. He made another beside the first, spread the edges apart, glimpsed the pole below, and dropped.

He landed on the pole and clung to it a moment, trying to hear past the beating of his heart. There was no stir below. He felt the cords around the pole, and began to pull up one bundle after another without troubling to open them, only cutting the cords and tying them together in pairs, in order to hang the bundles over the pole again until he was ready for them. When he had as many bundles as he could easily carry, that is to say, six, for the smallest was as big as his head and the largest four times that size, he began to think of his lost possessions, his leg thongs and the cloth which was all he had left of his treasures, except for some jewels in the magic jug. He did not include the box in this account, for it had betrayed him once and that was enough. He squatted on the pole looking down and listening. His eyes were now so accustomed to the dimness that he could make out a faint glow here and there. A vague bulk to one side must be the topmost platform, and remembering that this was empty, he dropped to it and paused to listen again. He heard the sound of faint steady breathing below. With sword in hand, he lowered himself to the next platform, and saw the bodies of demons lying sprawled all about him. By their size and number he knew these for the males; he saw their sharp sticks leaning in bundles against the wall.

The next platform was that of the children and females, and below that the lowest platform, with nothing on it but baskets and mats. From this he dropped to a pole, and so to the bottom. The floor of the chamber was deserted, except for one old female who lay near the wall and did not stir. In the gloom, something hung from the lowest pole which at first he did not recognize: then he saw that it was the talking box. He was afraid it might speak to him, but it did not. He prowled around the wall of the chamber, turning over scraps of rubbish, feeling inside baskets and under mats.

He found one of his thongs almost at once, lying as if dropped carelessly on the floor. There was no trace of the cloth, though he turned over every mat except the one the old woman was lying on. As he turned away in frustration the hanging box caught his eye, and in the dim light reflected from its side he saw a series of long scratch-marks. Had the demons hung the box there, then, to torment it in his stead? So much the worse for it. . . . Still, if he took the box, he would be thwarting the demons of their pleasure. He approached and put his hand on the cord the box hung by, and only then realized that it was his other leg-thong.

He rose to the pole and untied the thong, then retied it as a carrying loop, and with the box on his back climbed to the top of the chamber again. The sleeping demons did not stir as he passed.

Clinging to the crossbar under the roof, he thought of them sleeping peacefully. Bright light was what they hated; if he were to pull off the top of their house . . . but then the sound would awaken them. He touched the wall with his hand. Some of the woven fronds in the dome were new, but others were old and dry as tinder. Thorinn gathered up his bundles thoughtfully, dreaming of brightness. He leaped for the slit he had made and pulled himself through into daylight. Kneeling on the brown dome, he took the fire stick from his wallet and crumbled into it a few shreds of fiber pulled from the dome. One stroke set them aglow: he blew on them cautiously until a tiny pale flame leaped up, then tipped them out into a little pile of shredded fibers. After a few moments the flame caught, began to spread. Thorinn fed it with bits of brown leaf pinched off between his fingers, then with larger ones, then with whole strips carved out with his sword. A breath of foul air came up from the demons' den, making the fire burn more briskly. It popped, sending out sparks. Pungent whitish smoke billowed up. Bits of flaming tinder were dropping through the hole. Thorinn heard a shout of alarm below, then the tree began to shake. He cut a last strip, held the tip of it in the flames until it caught, then dropped it carefully into the blackness. He leaped to the topmost branches and from there swung out under the sky. Behind him gray-white smoke was spreading like a greasy cloud, and through it he could see the red glow of the fire like a demon's eye. He reached the hanging cord without difficulty, climbed up smiling, opened the shield, and let it close behind him.

8

How Thorinn was made captive by a flying engine that carried him deeper into the Underworld.

When he opened one of the bundles he had taken from the demons' house, he discovered that it contained lumps of dried meat, tough and nourishing. He ate his fill, drank water from the jug, then wrapped the meat again and put it away. Next he set the magic box upright on the floor and looked at it in silence awhile.

"Box," he said at last.

"I am here."

"Well, what have you got to say for yourself?"

"I have nothing to say for myself."

"Then why did you betray me?"

"What does betray mean?"

"Why did you tell them to use the sword on me, instead of—" Indignation choked him.

"I did not tell them to use the sword on you."

"Don't lie!"

"What does lie mean?"

"Not to tell the truth. Not to say what really happened."

"I tell only the truth."

"What a lie! Didn't you tell them the sword was better than a stick to cut with?"

"Yes."

"And didn't you know they would use it on me?"

"Yes."

"Well, then, why did you do it?"

"Because they asked."

Thorinn sat back on his heels, confused and angry. "If it happened again, would you do the same thing?"

"Yes."

"Tell them about the sword, and let them kill me with it?"

"Yes."

"Well then, don't you see, I can't have you with me any more, it wouldn't be safe." Thorinn stood up.

"It would be safe."

"How's that?"

"If you told me not to tell them the sword is better than a stick to cut with."

Thorinn squatted again, staring at the box. "You mean if I told you not to, you wouldn't?"

"Yes, I mean I wouldn't."

"Well— Suppose I tell you now never to do anything or say anything that will be bad for me. Does that mean you never will?"

"I never will."

"All right then," said Thorinn, "but I don't understand you. I don't care if you're a spirit or an engine, why should I have to tell you a thing like that?"

"An engine can only do as it is told," said the box.

"Do as I tell you, then," said Thorinn. After a moment he gathered his bundles together, slung them over his shoulder, box and all, and set off down the passage.

After a time the dark eye at the end of the tunnel suddenly blinked light, and Thorinn knew they had come to a shaft. Here he paused, for if the shaft went both up and down, he would have no choice but to go down it.

"Box, does that shaft go both ways?"

"Yes."

"Is there another shaft near here that only goes up?"

"What is near here?"

"Oh—within ten thousand ells?"

"No."

While he mulled this over, Thorinn set down his burdens, opened one of the meat packages and began to eat. Presently he said, "Box."

"Yes."

"You said that an engine can only do what it's told."

"Yes."

"But doesn't that mean that if I tell you to do one thing, and then later somebody else tells you just the opposite, you'd have to do what they told you and not me?"

"Not if you had told me not to obey them."

"Then if somebody asked you to tell them how to kill me, you wouldn't?"

"No, because you have told me not to do anything that would harm you."

"Are you sorry you did it before?"

"What does sorry mean?"

Thorinn tried to explain this, without much success, for the box did not know the meaning of "wish," and he had to explain that, and then "feeling," which the box could not seem to grasp at all. Finally it said, "Is being sorry wanting a thing to be different even though it has already happened?"

"Yes, I suppose so. Well, are you sorry?"

"No, because that would be senseless."

"How, senseless?"

"A thing that has already happened can't be made different. Therefore to want to make it different is senseless."

Thorinn was not content with this, and they argued the point a little longer, but neither could convince the other; the box would admit only that human beings could think in a way which was senseless if it pleased them, but that boxes could not.

"If I told you to think in what you call a senseless way, could you do it?"

"Yes, but then my thinking would not be good, and that would be bad for you."

"What about my thinking? Do you mean you think better than I do?"

"Yes."

Thorinn absorbed this in silence. "Box," he said presently, "you told me there were people at the bottom of the Underworld. Did you mean they are people like me, or gods and demons?"

"What are gods and demons?"

"Gods are—they are like men sometimes but they can take other shapes and you can't kill them. And demons the same but not as powerful."

"There are some people like you and some gods and demons at the bottom of the Underworld."

"Suppose I went there—could I steal some of their magic?"

"What is it to steal?"

"To take something that belongs to someone else."

"You could steal some things, and they would give you some things."

Thorinn was silent awhile. "The engines you talked about—would they take me there and not harm me?"

"Yes, Thorinn."

"And then would they take me back to the Midworld?"

"Yes, Thorinn."

"Could one of them come here?"

"Yes, if you call it." The crystal lighted, and Thorinn saw a tiny picture of himself bending over one of the rings in the tunnel, pressing it down. The ring sank into the floor. The box went dark.

"If I do that, the engine will come?"

"Yes."

"But why didn't you ever say so before?"

"You didn't ask."

Thorinn opened his mouth and shut it again. After a moment he said carefully, "If you had told me about the engine before, it would have helped me. Therefore by not telling you harmed me, do you see?"

"Yes, Thorinn."

"Well, then, after this you are not to harm me in that way any more. Do you understand?"

"Yes, Thorinn."

He was about to turn away when the crystal lighted; in it he saw a drop of water hanging from the end of a tube. It dropped, and yet remained in the middle of the crystal, and then grew larger as if he were moving closer to it. "In a drop of water there are many invisible things," said the box. The drop had swelled now to fill the crystal, and Thorinn saw that there were tiny swimmers in it, some with many legs, some with none, but all transparent as ice. "These creatures are too small to be seen with the eye; yet inside them are other things smaller still." In the crystal, one of the swimming things had grown huge, and inside it Thorinn could see a pulsing swarm of other creatures. He was interested, but after a few moments he began to grow impatient. The box went on showing him smaller and smaller things, until it got to a cluster of lights turning slowly against a dark background.

"Box, why are you showing me all this?"

"Because it is harmful to you not to know it." In the crystal, one of the lights had grown big, and now it separated into a central light and an outer shell. "All things are made up of these small pieces," said the box.

"That may be," said Thorinn, "but I don't see what it has to do with making the engine come."

"It has nothing to do with it, except that the engine also is made of these small pieces."

"All right then, tell me later." Thorinn retreated to the nearest light-ring. "Now, if I press down on this, the engine will come?"

"Yes."

"And it will not harm me?"

"No."

Thorinn took a long breath. There was something about this that he liked very little. Nevertheless he leaned, put his hand flat on the edge of the ring and pressed tentatively downward. Nothing happened. He pushed harder, but succeeded only in pressing himself away from the ring. At length, leaning both hands on the ring and throwing his weight forward, he felt the metal give. The whole ring, or at any rate the part of it he could see, sank into the floor of the tunnel, then slowly rose again. His weight was so little that he could not hold it down.

"Thorinn, I must ask you a question."

"Yes?"

"What is good for a man?"

"Why—I don't know, not being hurt or killed, I suppose, and not being sick, and having enough to eat. And living a long time, and having adventures, and becoming rich."

"What is having adventures?"

"Oh, meeting dangers and overcoming them."

"But in meeting dangers it is possible to be hurt or killed, and to be sick, and not to have enough to eat. And if a man is killed when he is young, then he cannot live a long time and may not become rich."

"That may be so, but a man must live like a man, or what's the point?"

"I don't know, Thorinn."

They waited until Thorinn's muscles began to grow stiff. He was beginning to realize again that he was hungry and thirsty. He unwrapped his pack and ate. When he had finished and drunk from the jug, he stood up and looked both ways along the tunnel. "The engine is not coming," he said.

"Shall I tell you more about the small pieces that all things are made from?" asked the box.

"No. You were wrong about the engine," said Thorinn with some satisfaction, and he picked up the box and slung it over his shoulder. Now he had to decide which way to go. The more he thought about it, the less he liked the idea of faring to the bottom of the Underworld. It would take him long enough as it was to get back to the Midworld, even if he could manage to go upward in spite of the geas. His best hope, it seemed to him, was to find some passage that went slanting up and down, always more up than down; the geas had never prevented him from using such passages.

He turned away from the shaft intersection and began loping down the tunnel. What if there were no shaft within ten thousand ells that led up and not down? Somewhere there must be one, and eventually he would find it.

Presently he thought he saw a flicker of light in the center of the eye of darkness at the end of the tunnel. He stopped to look at it, and in a moment he was sure: the winking dot was just perceptibly larger, brighter. The box said abruptly, "The engine is coming."

"I see it," said Thorinn, setting down his burdens. The dot swelled to a tiny circle. In the circle was a shape he could not quite make out. It did not look like one of the smooth eggs the box had shown him; it was angular, spiny. The flickering of the light-rings became visible as the thing swelled nearer.

"It is the wrong kind of engine," said the box suddenly. "It may be bad for you, Thorinn."

Thorinn stared wildly around. The shaft intersection was too far away; there was no place to run. Carrying his bundles, he ran up the smooth curve of the tunnel, leaped, clung to the side of the nearest light-ring. His bundles and the talking box hindered him, and he pushed them out of the way, but not before he saw a vast shape come drifting up the tunnel with dust fountaining under it. It had clusters of lights, great blank eyes, half-folded hands with pincers at the ends of them. He flattened himself to the wall behind the ring. The great shape darted past him in a cloud of dust. A few hundred ells beyond, it slowed and settled to the floor. All its eyes seemed to be in front. Thorinn cautiously slid himself over the top of the ring, pulled his bundles after, and flattened himself to the wall as before.

There were faint sounds and movements beyond, sighing of air, clicks, then a grating noise. Thorinn guessed that the thing was looking about to see what had pressed the ring down.

Silence. Thorinn held his breath, listening. A gray shape loomed over the ring, then a light, and another, and another. Thorinn sprang up in alarm. He got his good leg under him, kicked as the gray pincers taller than himself came forward. The thing tilted away from him, and he saw that it was a hollow structure of metal tubes, open above but with a complexity of solid parts below, the arms, pincers, lights, and eyes all attached to a sort of shield. The pincers loomed toward him.

When he awoke, he was in a moving place and his head hurt. He felt confused and tired, and it was easier to lie where he was, on a narrow bed, than to get up and worry about it. Beyond a large square-cornered window, the tunnel wall streamed past swiftly and smoothly; the room swayed a little. He closed his eyes.

Presently he felt better and sat up, but then he was dizzy and he sat cross-legged on the bed with his head in his hands. The bed was a narrow pallet on the floor. The smooth, rapid motion of the room continued.

He raised his head and looked around. At the back of the room there was a dark green basin with water trickling into it. His pallet was along one side, with another window over it which he had not noticed before. On the gray floor lay his bundles, the talking box, and his sword. Light came from a square of crystal in the ceiling.

There were two round crystals in the front wall, also, but they were dark.

He lurched to the basin, knelt, and drank until he could hold no more, then splashed a little water on his face. Beside the basin was a round hole in the floor. There was an odd smell in the room, like the stale of wild animals. Still feeling dizzy, he went back to the cot and sat down.

"Box," he said. "What happened?"

"The engine made you sleep and took you."

" 'Took me.' What do you mean? Took me captive, I suppose."

"Yes, took you captive. Then that engine took you to a place where it met this engine, and put you in it, still sleeping."

Thorinn considered all this, fuzzily. He felt that he should be frightened, but he was not, only interested. "Where is it taking me?" he asked.

"I don't know."

Thorinn shut his eyes and thought. He remembered the engine coming at him with its pincers wide, lights and eyes blazing—then nothing; try as he would, he could not remember the rest. "How did it put me to sleep?"

"It made a kind of air that puts men to sleep when they breathe it." The box began showing him a picture of the engine, and then of smaller and smaller parts of it, but Thorinn said, "Later." With an effort, he leaned over to pick up the sword in its scabbard and tried to put it through his belt; but that was too much trouble, and he laid it on the pallet. Beyond the window, the light-rings of the tunnel flashed by. If he followed one with his eyes for an instant, he could see it before it disappeared, but otherwise they all blurred together. Yet there was no wind. With another effort, he turned and put his hand to the window over his cot. It was filled with a sheet of crystal so clear that he could not see it. "Box," he said, "you've been the death of me."

The box was silent.

"Why did you tell me the engine would take me safely to the bottom?"

"When I was made, that was true."

Thorinn turned this over in his mind and could make nothing of it. "Why isn't it true now, then?"

"I don't know."

"Then what use are you?"

"I can turn one talk into another talk. I can answer questions about things that are not different since I was made. I can show pictures. I can—"

"Enough," said Thorinn. "Leave me alone now, can't you?"

"Yes, Thorinn." The box fell silent.

Thorinn got up and eased himself above the round hole in the floor, and drank more water, and lay down again. Presently he slept. When he awoke, he was hungry and his wounds throbbed. He ate some of the meat from his bundles and drank from the basin. He tried a little of the fruit he had brought, but it was rotting and he threw it down the hole. He felt anxious and tight; whatever it was that had made him sleepy before seemed to have worn off. He noticed a thin crack in the wall, outlining an upright oblong beside the window across the room, and realized for the first time that it must be a door. Above it was a curious set of complicated shapes nested into one another; after staring at this for some time with growing uneasiness, Thorinn realized that it resembled nothing so much as a pair of metal arms and pincers, like those of the engine that had captured him. A little later he noticed a second, smaller pair down at the other end of the room. Unfolded, by the look of them, the two sets of metal arms would be able to reach into any part of the room. There was nothing to hide behind—nothing moveable in the room, except his own belongings and the thin pallet, which was too flimsy to be of any use. Thorinn crossed the room and tried to wedge the point of his sword into the crack around the door, then into the space between two pieces of one of the metal arms, but without success. He returned to the cot.

"Box, how long have we been traveling?"

"We have been traveling for half a day and the sixth part of a day."

Thorinn tried to puzzle this out and gave up. "How far have we come?"

"We have come two thousands of thousands of ells and eight hundreds of thousands of ells."

Thorinn whistled. "How much farther are we going, then?"

"I don't know."

"What do you know?"

"I know this animal and this, and this plant"—pictures appeared in the crystal as it spoke—"and this, and this, and this engine"—a tangle of metal rods—"and this plant, and—"

"Peace," said Thorinn wearily. "When I ask you a question like that, don't answer."

The box fell silent. Presently Thorinn felt something pulling him forward, and the light-rings began to move more slowly past the windows. The rings widened and receded, and he had just time to realize that they had come to a junction where the tunnel met a shaft, when there was a lurch and the rings tilted in a dizzying fashion. Thorinn sat down abruptly, feeling heavier than he had since he had left the Midworld, then heavier still. When he was able to lift his head again, the light-rings outside were flickering downward past the window. After a minute or so, he felt himself growing lighter again, but the wall of the shaft remained blurred. He became as light as he had been before, then even lighter. He felt himself drifting away from the floor, and clutched vainly for something to hold onto. The box and his other belongings were floating into the air, as if they were all falling together—but the evidence of his eyes told him the engine was rising.

"Box," he cried, "what's happening?"

"We have stopped moving faster. The engine and everything in it are falling with the same quickness, therefore there is nothing to hold them together."

The room was slowly drifting around Thorinn in a lopsided circle, while the box and his bundles pursued different directions. Thorinn reached for one of the bundles as it floated by and caught it by the cord, but when he pulled, all that happened was that the bundle came to him, bounced off his chest, and began drifting lazily away again, while the room took on a different rotation.

"Box, I don't understand," said Thorinn. "How can we be falling up?"

"We are not falling up, we are falling down."

With a retort on his lips, Thorinn glanced out the window and saw that it was true—the light-rings of the shaft were blurring upward, while the room and all in it, *upside down,* fell toward the bottom of the Underworld. He made a wild grab at the bundle, which struck him a light blow on the forehead. When he looked again, the shaft wall had soundlessly reversed itself and was flowing downward. He shut his eyes in helpless misery. When he opened them, nothing had changed except that the box had drifted closer and the bundles farther away. "Box," he said.

"Yes, Thorinn."

"What will happen when we hit the bottom?"

"We will not hit the bottom."

"Why not?"

"We will slow down and go into one of the tunnels."

And afterward? The metal arms would unfold, the pincers would seize him. . . . The two crystals in the front wall, Thorinn realized suddenly, must be the eyes of the engine. If he could blind it somehow, then get the door open. . . . He thought of smearing the eyes with rotten fruit, and wished he had not thrown it down the hole. He could break the eyes perhaps, with his sword, if he could get near enough. The bundle he had had before had drifted out of reach. He closed his eyes again.

At length he roused—something was happening. The floor, which had somehow swung under him, drifted nearer. He touched, got his balance, stood erect. The box and the bundles lay on the floor nearby.

"Have we stopped?" Thorinn asked, but in the next moment he saw it was not so: the light-rings in the shaft outside were flickering past as swiftly as before.

"No," said the box.

"Then why do we have weight again?"

"Because the engine is no longer moving as the earth pulls it—it is moving at one speed and no faster, although the earth pulls it to move faster."

"And that makes us have weight?"

"It makes us have the feeling of weight."

"Weight is weight," said Thorinn after a moment.

"No, because when you put some small thing on your open hand and then turn, swinging your arm very fast"—the crystal lighted as it spoke, and there was a very small Thorinn whirling with his arm extended—"the thing presses against your hand and does not fall. That is not weight, but it is the feeling of weight."

Thorinn, to his surprise, began to feel that he understood this. He talked idly with the box awhile longer, then lay down on the pallet with his hands under his head. He must have slept, for when he opened his eyes he sensed a change. He stood up. The light-rings of the shaft outside were moving more and more slowly, another proof that the box was right. There was a lurch, the shaft wall swung toward them, and Thorinn sat down involuntarily on the floor, while the box and his bundles slid toward the back of the room. Thorinn got his sword as it went by and waited for the pull to stop. When it did, a few minutes later, he was caught off guard but scrambled upright anyway.

He would have to strike quickly twice, and break both the eyes of the engine. He leaped, and remembered nothing more.

9

How Thorinn tried to cross a river, and found it unlike other rivers.

3892 A.D.:

Having been advised to undertake some unnecessary and intricate study, I chose languages, and for my first attempt selected Lower Southwest Emmish, since my business requires me to visit that sector frequently. At first I found the subject tiring in the extreme, but persevered, and after several months began to acquire some facility. The chief difficulty I found was not in learning the words themselves or their manner of pronunciation, although this included mastering several unaccustomed sounds, but—and this was wholly unexpected—in learning the order in which the words are made into sentences and the ways in which they influence one another. The translator had no rules governing these things in its memory, but at my order was able to deduce and formulate them; this aided me considerably, but many difficulties remained unresolved.

To give an example of the simplest kind, where we say, "I intend to take some rest now," the Loswem says (literally translated), "Being at repose this one is to call." At first I believed

*that there must be some malfunction in the translator, but a sec-
ond machine gave me identical results, and later I was able to ob-
serve that when a Loswem expressed a desire translated as "I intend to take some rest now," this in fact was what he actually said.
I commented to a professional acquaintance of mine that I wondered how he could express himself in so illogical and arbitrary a
language; he at first pretended not to know what I meant, and
when at length I made him understand, by showing how much
more clearly and simply we convey the same meaning, he expressed the opinion that it was our language which was illogical
and unwieldy. From this I began to suspect that all languages may
be almost equally arbitrary and illogical, although some, such as
Loswem, are certainly more so than others. In the course of my
discussion with my acquaintance, before he tired of the subject, I
found that it was impossible to translate the word "intend" into
his language at all; when I asked the translator to do it, it replied
that it could not do so without the context.*

*As I advanced in facility I was able to understand more and
more of what my Loswem acquaintances said, though not to express myself to them in their tongue: they claimed not to understand me, and could not see the point of making the effort when a
translator was at hand. I would have abandoned the undertaking,
since several of my acquaintances were beginning to regard me as
mentally disturbed, but I felt impelled to continue, though more
discreetly, as a consequence of certain discoveries which seemed
to me sinister. I discovered, in fine, that in all but the simplest ut-
terances, the Loswem original differed in meaning, sometimes substantially, from the translator's version. This became particularly
evident in all discussions concerning religion, local customs, mar-
riage and family life, etc. To give an example of this, in listening
to a recorded political conference between our representatives and
theirs early in the year just past (in Loswem, obtained while
there), I heard the translator say, "We must safeguard our territo-
rial integrity," a familiar Loswem statement, but the speaker in
fact had remarked (literally translated), "It requires itself that we
others in no way mix our sacred blood," which is an entirely
different thing. I found numerous other examples, and the more I
pondered over them, the more I came to believe that the political
differences between us, which grow daily more exacerbated, are
due to these mistranslations, for which, however, the translators*

cannot be blamed, since they are inherent in the nature of the two languages: and when this is compounded by the number of separate languages spoken in the world—I believe it is more than three thousand—the situation can only be seen as extremely grave. Yet the solution, if there is one, eludes me. The mobility of modern life requires that we come into constant contact with those who speak other languages, and it would be impossible for all of us to learn each other's tongues; in fact, without the invention and wide use of the translator, modern civilization would be impossible. The problem would be solved if everyone were to learn a single language, but if we cannot even agree with Loswem on the salinity of their efferent water, what chance have we of imposing the simplest and most convenient of all languages—our own, of course—on the whole world with its two hundred billion people?

For a long time he lay hearing the roar of water. Sometimes he lost interest and stopped attending to it, but when he came back again it was always there, distant, muted and not unpleasant. At intervals a large cold drop fell on his face or hand. He did not seem able to turn or cover his face, but this was not alarming, and in fact he forgot about it each time until the next drop reminded him. He opened his eyes, saw nothing but grayness, and closed them again. Presently the world grew lighter beyond his closed lids. He felt there was something he should remember, but could not. He opened his eyes and managed to sit up; he was dizzy and his head hurt. Now he remembered the other time, and he looked around for the box and his other belongings. They were all there, lying beside him on a sloping wet shelf of stone. The air was full of tiny droplets, and the stone was spattered with larger ones that fell now and again; his shirt and breeks were dripping, and he felt damp all over. Before him in the silvery light was a wide gray pool into which a curtain of water descended with a continual roar. The surface of the pool was boiling white; droplets flew and drifted in every direction. Waves surged up unceasingly on the shelf, breaking upon a few bare sticks that lay there. Behind him was a wet wall of rock, hollowed out and overhanging the shelf; what was above that he could not see. A few trailing ferns grew in the crannies of the rock, and there was moss deep in the recess.

When he tried to stand, he found himself so light that he overbalanced at once; his feet floated up while his head and shoulders

went down. He tried again, steadying himself against the rock wall
this time, and managed to stay up, though his foot on the wet
stone had a disposition to drift out from under him. It cost him
more effort and several absurdly slow falls to gather up his
belongings and hang them about his shoulders. At length it occurred to him to take off his shoes and put them into his belt. Bare
toes gave him better footing, and he began to work his way
around the recess. As he followed the curve, the recess narrowed
and he saw a strip of misty light at the end of the falling water.
The rock shelf narrowed here, too, then pinched out altogether.
There was nothing for it but to wade in the shallow water, on the
submerged stone that was so slippery that he went down instantly
in slow motion, floundered up and drifted down again, among
white sprays of water that hung unnaturally in the air before they
curved over and dripped to the surface again. Individual droplets
fell in front of his nose, and he could see them changing shape as
they moved—they were not teardrops as he had always supposed,
but globes that were constantly deformed this way and that, pulsing and trembling as they fell. Thorinn watched them in amazement, too fascinated to think of getting up until they had all
dropped into the water, each leaving its tiny peak and then subsid-
ing among its slow ripples.

He found that the only way he could make any progress at all
was to remain on all fours, not even crawling but hitching himself
forward with sudden jerks of his arms and knees. Surges of water
flung themselves at his face, and he had to close his mouth and
eyes until they had struck and dripped slowly away. In this manner he moved forward a few ells, feeling like a drowned worm,
until a gravel beach appeared between the cliff and the water.
Here he could stand again, and next came a jumble of boulders
that was even better. He was wet through, and cold—it was colder
here than anywhere he had been in the Underworld, and it struck
him now that it might be true after all about the regions of eternal
ice at the bottom of the world. As he moved forward, he could see
vague shapes in the mist that might have been trunks of slender
trees. Remembering his experience with the demons, he went cautiously, pausing often to listen. The boulders decreased in size;
bare earth began to appear between them, then a tangle of damp
stalks and vines. Out of prudence Thorinn stopped and put his
shoes on, but the footing here was almost as bad as in the water,

and he had to go on his belly again, gripping the vines to draw himself forward. This was a better way of moving than any he had found yet, and he could have moved faster still were it not that he was alarmed by the way his body floated away from the ground whenever he pulled too vigorously.

Something dark lay athwart his path. Thorinn approached it cautiously and found it was a dead tree-trunk, spongy and half rotten. The peeling bark was reddish-gray, like that of a larch, but it was divided into vertical segments with pointed tops and bottoms. Although he was shivering with cold, Thorinn suppressed the impulse to build a fire. He passed the log and went on up the slope, avoiding the upright shapes—they appeared to be limbless trees, in fact, but the last thing he wanted was to climb a tree whose top was invisible.

The mist thinned as he ascended, and the wall of the cliff came into view again. It was bare reddish-brown rock for the most part, with only an occasional trace of green. Brambles pricked his fingers, and once he heard something small go scurrying off in the ground-cover. Otherwise the world seemed to be empty, and the going was so easy that he covered several hundred ells in a few minutes; but the exercise was not enough to warm him.

The mist had thinned to such an extent that when he stood beneath one of the trees and gazed up, he could see all the way to the top where a spray of branches erupted at last from the straight trunk. He embraced the tree and rose almost without effort, gliding upward with the trunk between his legs; in a few moments, to his elation, he found himself high above the mist. The slope where he had been crawling moments ago was covered with a white blanket, dissolving at the top into trailing wisps. Around him the dark staffs of the trees stood erect and still; beyond them he could see the cataract and hear it, too, better than before. The white band fell straight into the mist, twenty ells away from the rock wall; he followed it upward until his neck cracked, but could not see the top; it was lost in sky-glare and haze.

Turning the other way, he looked out over a steeply descending countryside dappled with mist in the hollows. He could see a river emerging from the mist around the cataract; it vanished between two hills, but farther off it reappeared in vast shining loops. A flash of pale brown caught his eye—it was a bird winging slowly away in the distance. Far down the valley, blue with haze, he could see a cluster of spires that looked like the work of men; otherwise, across the whole landscape, there was no sign of life—no movement, no buildings or livestock, not a thread of smoke. He released his hold on the tree and began to drift downward, so slowly that he lost patience and propelled himself faster with his hands. Once on the ground, he began to crawl upslope again. As soon as he had climbed above the mist line, he turned away from the cataract and began to parallel the river.

The ground cover was made up of things that looked like vines and grasses but were neither. Some ended in drooping bundles of leaves, like little besoms; others bore tiny purple blossoms. To all appearance it was early spring here, although it had been full summer when he left Hovenskar. How long had he been gone? He put his back against a fallen tree-trunk and began to count on his fingers. He had slept once in the tunnel and three times in the first cavern, the one where he had lost his sword and regained it. In the second cavern he had spent a long time, perhaps as much as twenty days. He had slept once in the treasure cavern, twice while falling down the shaft, once (but probably not long) in the third cavern where the demons had tormented him, then six or seven days in the cavern above that, and once in the engine, and once here. The most he could make of it was thirty-seven days.

"Box," he said, as he unwrapped one of his bundles of food, "how is it that it's spring here but summer in Hovenskar?"

"Here and Hovenskar are two different places."

"I know that. What I mean is—oh, never mind." He took a bite of meat and chewed moodily. In fact, he didn't know what he did mean. Why shouldn't it be spring in one place and summer in another?

"Box, how can I get out of this place?"

"By going through the falling water."

"The waterfall, you mean? Is that how we got in?"

"Yes. There is no other way."

"How do you know that?"

"If there were another way to get out, the engine would not have brought you here. It would have taken you to another place where there was no other way to get out. Therefore in this place there is no other way to get out."

"All right, enough," said Thorinn, and sat awhile in silence. He was puzzled about the box. On certain subjects it seemed perfectly

A hollow structure of metal tubes . . . (p. 101)

Thorinn began counting the wingmen as they were revived. (p. 129)

Now he could see the two engines with their noses against the bladder
... (p. 151)

. . . a man in a white robe was standing there. (p. 169)

sensible, but on others it could talk nothing but nonsense. It
seemed to be saying now that the engine had brought him here to
imprison him—but why?

"Box," he said presently, "could you teach me to make an engine that would take me up out of this place?"

"Yes, Thorinn."

In the crystal, a tiny Thorinn stood on a peg that jutted from
the cliff face beside the cataract. With a hammer he drove another
peg into the cliff above his head, then pulled himself up to stand
on it. "What are those pegs made of?" Thorinn asked, leaning
closer.

"Of metal."

"Spikes, you mean, then. But where am I to get the metal to
forge such spikes? And the hammer to drive them?"

"I don't know." The crystal flickered; now Thorinn was hanging from a huge bladder that drifted through the air just under the
sky.

"What is that bladder made of?"

"Leather."

"What makes it float that way?"

"It is full of a gas that is lighter than air."

"But where am I to get such a gas?"

"I don't know." The crystal flickered again, but Thorinn said,
"Never mind," and rolled away from the box.

From the crest of the next hill he had a glimpse of the river far
below. Instead of trying to walk down the slope, he lay on his
belly and began to pull himself downhill with his fingers. In a few
moments the trees began to thin out; then they were behind him
and he was soaring down into a wide yellow-green valley. The
angle of his descent and the pitch of the hillside were so perfectly
matched that he found himself floating like a bird just above the
grasstops, and it almost seemed that he could go on forever; then
the floor of the valley came up, grasses whipped his face, and he
was skidding to rest, deep in the wet grass.

He climbed the next hill. It was a little warmer on the crest, and
why that should be he did not know, for the skylight gave no
heat. The air was mild and still. Below him he could see the river
glinting between wooded banks, then another ridge and another,
until the landscape was lost in haze.

There was something odd about the river, but he could not

make it out because of the intervening brush and trees. Thorinn pulled himself down the hill on his belly as before. The trees at the river's edge rose up around him, and now he saw what was peculiar about the river itself—it ran here at such a steep angle that it should have been brawling and leaping, but instead it lay perfectly smooth. Looking at it made him feel dizzy at first, as if he were about to lose his balance.

He pulled himself through the tangle of underbrush and stood on the bank. Now he could see one or two faint arrowhead markings where the current ran over snags far out in the river; except for these, he would not have known that the water was moving at all. He dropped a dead leaf in, saw it drift, touch, and move leisurely away. He threw a stone in to see how deep the water was, and raised a white splash almost as high as his head. It slowly collapsed, leaving a ring of irregular drops that followed, and as slowly a central spout grew out of it; then that collapsed too, leaving an unsteady globe, all with dreamlike slowness, while a second ring of pale water began to form around the first, traveling outward as it grew; then a third inside where the central spout had been, and as they traveled sedately after one another, a fourth began. The central globe and the droplets where they fell raised other splashes, not so tall as the first, and from these shallow rings spread out, crossing the bigger ones in a way that made Thorinn dizzy to watch. The first splash had been ragged, but the traveling rings were pure shapes of transparent water, each with a shine of reflected skylight at its lip. They were beautiful, and in their descending heights as they went outward there was a curve that was beauty too. Each wave died away when it reached an invisible circular line an ell or so from the center, and this line was moving outward as well, but not as fast as the waves, so that they continually overtook it and died. And moment by moment the marching waves were less tall, till at last they were only ripples breaking against the river bank, each returning its reflection; then the river was smooth again.

After a time Thorinn threw in another stone and again saw the pause, the sudden leap of water, the crown of droplets twisting and wavering as they slowly fell, the spreading rings like magical moving fortifications. In the tall ring-waves, suspended particles streamed up one side and down the other. The waves kept the same precise distance one from another: how did they do it?

Thorinn tried throwing in two stones at once, and saw to his amazement that the water rings passed through each other without resistance, throwing up a rounded peak at each crossing-point, and as the crossing-points moved, the peaks effortlessly moved with them and then disappeared. He had seen all this before, in the spring above Hovenskar, but there the waves had been so shallow and quick that he had never thought how mysterious they were.

A little farther downstream he found a shallow backwater where he stripped and bathed himself. The water leaped around him, stinging cold; afterward, he made a small fire at the water's edge, using bits of the driftwood that was heaped at the bend of the river. The flames curved out, blunt and pale, and although he added more fuel, they never rose much higher; it was as if some of the virtue had gone out of the wood.

A light rain began. He put on his clothes, covered the remains of his smoldering fire, and wandered abstractedly up the river bank, pulling himself along from one sapling to another. Presently the rain stopped and the city came into view, nearer than he had yet seen it, across the next reach of the river. Thorinn climbed a tree to look at it. Perhaps, he thought, the city was inhabited by nocturnal demons, like those who had tormented him in the other cavern, but he doubted it. It was something else: something was wrong. A brown bird passed overhead, almost invisible in the sky-glare. Below, the river was too wide to leap across. Thorinn climbed down and looked at it. Farther upstream the river might be narrow enough to jump, but it would take him too long to find out. He cut a long pole from a sapling and went looking for a log of deadwood.

He found one in a tangle of brush, a bare section of trunk two ells long with a smaller limb projecting at a narrow angle, like a big finger and a little finger. The limb, he thought, would make the log less likely to roll over and would save him the trouble of finding some way to lash two logs together. He dragged it into the shallows where it floated barely out of water; but as the trunk was curved there was a portion of it that stood higher than the rest, and Thorinn stepped aboard there with his pole. The log dipped majestically, lurched, rose again while a wave surged out knee-high all around him. He planted the pole on the bottom and pushed cautiously; the log seemed to move, but in the wrong direction, and Thorinn found himself toppling forward. He straightened up and tried again, and presently found that by leaning back against the pole he could make the log move in the direction he wished. The bottom sloped away until he was using half the length of the pole. Presently the current took him, but he had got the hang of it now—the trick was to keep the log moving against the water, for it was easiest to push when it was moving. With each stroke the forward end of the log rose and dipped, making a tall arrow-shaped wave and scattering a few balls of water the size of his fist that wabbled away bright in the skylight. A breeze sprang up, and gentle wavelets began to march past the log one after another. As the breeze freshened, the waves grew taller and farther apart. Thorinn realized with alarm that the log was already pitching dangerously. Up it went, standing almost upright, then tilted back as the next wave thrust under it. Now each wave had a white crest, and the air was full of water-balls that burst cold against his face. Desperately he kept his balance on the log, knowing that if he fell off he must drown. The pole hampered him and he let it go; the wave swung it back across his chest. It was not a heavy blow, but he realized that he could no longer feel the log with his feet. Half-blinded by spray, he saw the log lifting past him and clutched at it. Then he was in the water, with the slippery dead weight twisting in his arms. His head went under; cold water filled his ears, his nose, his mouth. He struggled, somehow found himself atop again, clutching the limb with one hand and the trunk with the other. He had time for one breath before the log tilted headlong down the next wave, down, down, until he thought it must go over; then he realized with horror that it *was* going over. The cold water strangled him; he clawed his way out of it up the trunk as it rose to the crest, pitched, began to slide down. Through the pelting drops of spray he had a blurred glimpse of the river and something gray-brown that moved overhead; then he was sliding down the wave again. A cross-wave tilted the log again and he was half in the water, choking. A lurch took them up again. Cold thoughts came into his head: if he let go the log he sank; if he clung to it he drowned. At the top of the surge, he balanced himself desperately atop the log, let go, and leaped away.

The river dropped below him, the whitecaps like the tops of spears. He could see the far shore, still a hundred ells distant. Now the river rose toward him again; through the flying spray he saw the log lurch upward, reached, grasped it, swung around with agonizing slowness, and went under. He came up drenched and half-blinded; he balanced himself again somehow on the plunging log and leaped once more, this time at an angle.

Raindrops were descending in long silver chains blown awry by the wind and mingled with the spray. The river rose again below him. The log was gone, and the shore. Now he saw the pebbled beach, but he would fall a dozen ells short of it. Down he went helplessly; the water sprang up over his chin and nose, then his good foot touched something and he leaped up, fighting for breath, down again, and he was in the shallows. He strove against the waves and in a moment staggered up alive onto the wet pebbles.

The wind slackened and died; the waves subsided. Presently the river was glassy smooth as before.

10

How Thorinn entered a town of seven towers, and dissolved
its enchantment by accident.

*The Egg has a shell of stone which is coexistent and immen-
surable. All other substances spring from and return to this shell.
The upper portion of the shell, or lucilacunar, is by turns bright,
that men may see, and dark, that they may rest. The lower portion, or solum, is covered with a layer of earth, from which all
rooted and crawling things arise; in which they are nourished in
their season; and to which they return so that others may be en-
gendered.*

The Abiotic Period. *In the Abiotic Period, which endured
immensurably until the beginning of Eobiotic times, the Egg was
empty, bare and dark. There was no life nor motion in it, nor was
any life or motion conceivable, possible or prefigurable.*

The Eobiotic Period. *At the opening of the Eobiotic Period,
nine dozen great gross years before the present era, the smooth
shell of the Egg became porous and pitted; this took six great
gross years. Following this, the porous stone exuded vapors which
became the air; this took eight great gross years. Next the stone*

crumbled and formed the solum, a process which took four great gross years; then angiosperms appeared both in the solum and in the lucilacunar; from these all other rooted and crawling things developed by anabasis and phylogeny. These processes consumed still another eight great gross years. In all, the Eobiotic Era lasted twenty-six great gross years.

The Paleobiotic Period. At the beginning of the Paleobiotic Period, the Egg was substantially as we know it, but there was no higher life. Higher life now emerged in the form of coelelminthes which perfused from the vesicles of the homunculolilium, or manlily. According to tradition, one of these coelelminthes, a worm named Rambatnib, declared himself ruler of the Egg. Taking as his consort another worm named Dola, he reigned for two great gross years. Among his many descendants were the helminthes, the coelenterates, and the rodents, one of whom, Palak by name, slew and deposed Rambatnib in the year 14,361. Palak and his consort Eula are credited with introducing the arts of music and weaving; hence the term palqu't *for a brief garment or clout, and* Palak-Eulalian Mode *for a kind of music no longer played. They reigned until 15,350, when one of Palak's grandsons, a watervole named Cletus, gathered an army and laid siege to the palace. Palak, who loved luxury, was surprised and slain in his bath by Cletus, who thereupon assumed the throne and declared a Great Gross Year. It was during Cletus's reign that the Nine Books and Three Oracles were composed and the Cletian Games instituted. In 16,153 Cletus awarded himself an epithet, "the Golden," by which he is still known in some chronicles, and in 16,790 he died under mysterious circumstances of which nothing is now known. After an interregnum, during which a flood carried away the treeposts of the Palace and its outworks, a convocation known as the Broad Meadow Assembly chose as their new monarchs a kingfisher called Wise and his wife, known as Yellow Hands.*

The Archaeobiotic Period. After reigning for seven great gross years, Wise determined to become a man, and henceforward was called Lembepatkin. He begged Yellow Hands to become a woman and remain his wife, but she refused and went down into the bullrushes, where her descendants hunt fish to this day. Lembepatkin took another wife, and ruled for three great gross years. He instituted the art of writing, reformed the Four Directions, and founded the Great College. He was succeeded by his son, Til-vebegarengen.

The Historical Period. *The first persons of whom authenticated written records have survived to the present day are two brothers named Om and Hem, who in the year 63,794 disputed the ruler-ship of the entire Egg, Om being then the monarch of the East Kingdom and Hem of the West. For a time the struggle was equal, but Om had an artificer called Firebringer who made for him certain devices, one of which was said to be a flame-breathing bladder, and another an artificial mole, which tunneling under the enemy's outworks caused great destruction. Seeing that the con-test went against him, Hem called on the services of another artificer, Redbird, who made for him comparable devices, and to-gether the brothers and their armies wrought such devastation in the Egg that after their final battle, in the autumn of 63,797, both kings and all their captains lay slain and all their works leveled to the ground. After another interregnum, the survivors and their descendants agreed never to use such instruments again in war or peace. An early religious poem of this period, the Song of Closing, movingly depicts the moral earnestness of the survivors by means of an allegory in which they seal up the walls of the Egg forever. In 63,893 the Great College was reconstituted and the treeposts erected for the present corpus of knowledge. The names of the Masters of the Great College, from that day to this, are Lobeck, Morblen, Binton, Winsin, Tenwin, Ponsin, Tenlon, Mistwin, Ben-lob, Finmor, Kinten, Tabeck, Vennkin, Windesh, Remten, Benrosh, Bistfin, Sinpast, Roshkin, Pongass, Sinmar, Pastwin, Tetheck, Wishchin, Deshton, Gasstab, Mistmass, Rishten, Bretlob, Friteck, Blenkot, Findesh, Klanchet, Bretsin, Gassplan, Menchet, Lobnet, Niteck, Finplan, Pastchet, Sinzet, Mistklan, Votmass, Lesteck, Dretbrin, Remfret, Tremnet, Winchet, Deshfin, Eckrosh, Tethdret, Wetklan, Findesh, Brinsin, Findesh, Gasstlin, Netmist, Lestnet, Wishteth, Roshnet. . . .*

Thorinn crawled under a bush, untied his bundles with shaking fingers, and slept. When he awoke, it was full green dark; he was wet and cold, and the wind was shaking droplets of water from the bush onto his face. For a moment he thought himself back in the cave behind the cataract; then he remembered, and sat up, shiver-ing. He tied his bundles around him and crawled out from under

the bush. The green skylight was too faint for walking, and he
climbed the nearest tree instead. From its tip, a hundred ells above
the ground, he could make out the clustered towers not far off in
the bend of the river. They were dark and still.

As he watched, a sudden bar of gold appeared at the end of the
cavern. It widened, swelled, grew paler; then it was sweeping overhead, and as it passed Thorinn glimpsed a brown bird wheeling
above, head cocked, one bright black eye looking down. The skylight dazzled him, and when he could see again the bird was gone.

He followed the river bank eastward awhile, then climbed the
slope and found himself in a plowed field. It had been planted to
beans, or some other garden vegetable, and the young shoots were
coming up half-covered by weeds. Nearer now, the towers were
surrounded by a huddle of smaller buildings. As he approached,
he could see that they were built around the trunks of young trees;
they appeared to be made of withy, and sometimes the green
branch of a tree peeped out to show that it was still there. Some of
the curving walls were plastered with a substance like pale mud,
others daubed with bright color in stripes and circles. Grasses and
weeds were sprouting in the earth around the buildings; there were
a few marks of hoofs and clawed feet, but none that looked re-
cent, and none that were human. The byres were vacant, doors
standing open.

The seven towers clustered in a crescent around a great courtyard overgrown with vines and grass. After the first two hundred
ells or so each tower was capped with a conical roof, but from this
roof sprang another, smaller tower, not from the peak of the roof
but to one side of it, and sometimes the roof of this tower, too,
sprouted still another tower. Buttresses joined the towers; some of
these had windows or even balconies in them.

Thorinn went on into the empty courtyard. He listened: not a
sound. From the balconies overhead hung vines with yellowed
leaves; there was a sweetish smell of decay in the air. Among the
litter between the buildings he found several jugs and drinking
vessels, a tunic of red woven cloth, curiously made with bone fas-
tenings at the sides; a broken framework of wood with some
parchmentlike substance stretched over it; a mirror of polished silver in a bone frame; and a little idol or godlet made of soft cloth,
with a gray button-eyed face and long naked wings like those of a
wingmouse.

He sprang up to the first balcony and peered within. The floor
was resilient, loosely woven of cords; there were a few low carved
tables, but no chairs or beds. The ceiling seemed extraordinarily
high; below it were rods that might have been perches for birds.

Beyond was a maze of other rooms, gloomy even by day.
Thorinn found a light-box on the wall, divided into two compart-
ments like his own, the moss in one compartment still feebly
alight. He transferred a pinch of it to the other compartment and
carried it into the next room, then set it down again; it made him
uneasy to be surrounded by such a bubble of light with darkness
beyond it. A few moments later, when he turned to look behind,
he saw the translucent partition dully glowing.

The rooms were arranged in a ring around a vast well in the
center of the tower, thirty ells across and at least two hundred
deep. Dim chinks of light, far up, illuminated it. The silence was
murmurous. Thorinn retreated into the rooms again.

Litter was everywhere, but no more than you would expect to
find in any household—clothing, scraps of this and that, things that
might have been children's toys carved of wood. In closets and
chests he found more clothing, all with the same curious side-fas-
tenings, hanging neatly or carefully folded; also cabinets full of
curious little wooden and bone implements, of whose use he had
no notion. The feeling was strong on him that the people who lived
here had only gone away for a while—but where could they have
gone?

Over most of the valley, the tall trees grew toward the tops of
the slopes, along the cavern walls; farther down there was scrub
and then meadow, with a few coppices here and there. Occasionally he found a tangle of brush and vines, compacted into a
single whorled mass with tunnels all through it, some of them
large enough to admit a man. He ventured into one of these, and
had crawled a dozen ells into a pleasant leafy gloom, when, as he
pulled himself around a bend, he heard a "Whuff!" and found
himself staring into a furry, big-eyed face almost as big as his own.
He was too astonished to think of drawing his sword, even if there
had been room in the tunnel; the beast turned and vanished, and
Thorinn, with some difficulty and many scratches, backed out
again.

Droppings were plentiful, from pellets the size of millet-grains

to chalky lumps the size of his fist. In the soft turf of the meadows and along the river bank he found the prints of sharp
hooves or claws, angled backward. One early morning he surprised a thing like a large hare, and knocked it over with a stone.
It got up and leaped off into the bushes, but not before he had
seen that its hind legs had blunt spiky claws, and that it leaped by
thrusting its toes into the ground.

Birds' eggs there were in plenty, in the treetops and in the reeds
along the river. The water birds mocked him with scornful honks,
a few ells away in the stream, but when they went ashore with
their webbed feet they were almost helpless; he lay in wait for
them in the rushes, caught them, and wrung their necks.

Three times more he climbed a tree just before dawn or nightfall, and three times he saw the same brown bird.

To pass the time, Thorinn let the box tell him more of its stories about how the world was made. There were little bits of matter, too small to see, and these bits themselves were made up of
smaller bits, and so on. Then there were things that were not solid
at all and could not be seen either, and with these things it was
possible to keep time from passing in certain places, so that, for
instance, the weight of the earth above a cavern in the Underworld
could not crush it, and also the heat of the lower parts of the earth
could be drawn off and kept until it was needed. For all these
things the box had outlandish words of its own, and it always told
the same stories concerning them, but it could not give any proof
that they were true, and Thorinn could not see what use it was to
know them.

As for the world itself, the box maintained that it was a great
ball, the Midworld being its surface, with a sort of tent all around
it to keep the air in. When Thorinn asked what was beyond that,
the box replied that it was a vast space like a cavern with no walls,
which nevertheless did not go on forever but had an end somewhere; and when Thorinn inquired what was beyond *that,* the box
replied that the question was senseless.

The box further maintained that the world was pushing itself
about in this enormous cavern by means of tubes which pierced
the tent and from which invisible particles were expelled. Snorri's
Pipe, it appeared, was one of these tubes, but just when Thorinn
thought he had understood this, and asked why the tubes had only

now begun to make the world go faster, the box replied that on the contrary, they were slowing it down.

He tried to teach the box a game of insults, which Withinga and Untha had often played in the evenings (though with them the game had never lasted long before one player lost his temper); but he could not seem to explain to the box what an insult was, and having to play both sides took the fun out of it.

Weary of walking on his toes and crawling in the underbrush, he cut a piece of deadwood with a projecting stub, flattened it with his sword and tied it to one shoe so that the stub was angled backward under the ball of his foot. Now he could leap as the hares and other animals did, though he could never catch them.

After the first few days he grew tired of sleeping in the wet forest, and moved into one of the tower rooms, a small chamber directly under the peak of the roof, where, he reasoned, he would have the most warning if the owners came back; it had a window through which he could escape quickly into the trees if necessary. He slept poorly here, and had bad dreams.

He awoke one morning with the fantastic notion that there were cellars under the city, with hidden trap doors, and that the tower people with all their children and livestock were hiding below. The feeling was so strong that he went and looked at the floors of the central shaft, and the byres and workshops, but they were solid packed earth, as he had known before. Yet, if the people and their animals were still in the cavern, they must be hidden underground. He felt them there, by day and night, dumb eyeless presences.

He explored the valley, first downstream, then up. Twice he found small steadings tucked away between the forest and the meadows, but they were as deserted as the city. At the far end of the valley, the river turned into a labyrinth of more and more sluggish waterways. Wading with poles in the marsh, Thorinn found that the water flowed under the cliff through a slot too narrow for a man.

For sport and to vary his diet, he took a bow and some arrows he had found in the city, and practiced shooting at a mark until he had lost all but two of the arrows in the brush. He had a tendency to shoot high, and supposed that was because the arrow, not being as heavy as it ought to be, fell too slowly in flight.

He fetched more arrows and continued to practice outdoors; he also hung a mark at the top of one of the inner wells in the city and shot at it from below. When he could hit this target more often than not, he threw it into the air and practiced shooting at it as it soared. He kept on, day after day, until he seldom lost an arrow, and could hit the target in flight nine times out of ten. Then one morning he got up before dawn and climbed a tree. Balancing himself on a limb just below the tip, he unbuckled his belt, passed it around the stem and refastened it. Now, leaning back against the belt, he could look upward without losing his balance or risking a sore neck.

In the treetops all around him, birds were making their morning noises. He waited.

The golden bar appeared at the end of the cavern, and he found time to wonder where the light came from that turned the dark sky-moss bright—did the sky of one cavern join that of another, all around the Underworld? He took an arrow from his quiver, nocked it, drew the bowstring back. The light swept overhead, and in the instant of its passage he clearly saw the brown bird. He released the arrow; it vanished silently into the glare, but he knew it had been truly aimed. He put another arrow to the bow and squinted upward. There! A dark shape gliding down, turning, crippled. He let fly, missed, nocked another arrow, released it, and this time saw it strike. The bird was pinwheeling slowly into the trees. Thorinn marked the spot where it vanished and scrambled down.

A rhythmic thrashing in the underbrush led him to his quarry. Transfixed by two arrows, in the body and in the wing, it lay tangled in spiky bushes, still trying to fly. One wing was crippled; the other flapped, flapped, flapped.

Thorinn bent nearer. It was a large bird, bigger than a hawk, but having a short, straight bill. Its feathers were dark brown above, buff below. Its bright eye stared fixedly past him; the beating of its wing neither quickened nor faltered. Thorinn drew his sword and struck. The blade rebounded; the bird's neck was bent but not cut through, and there was no blood. The rhythmic flapping continued. Thorinn struck again, with no better result. Finally, conquering his revulsion, he pulled the thing out into a clear spot, where, holding it against a fallen log, he chopped with his sword until he had cut the neck half through and opened a gash in the body beneath the crippled wing. Cut feathers drifted away in the wind of his blows, but still the bird did not bleed. At last the flapping stopped. Inside the body Thorinn saw unfamiliar dry shapes, unlike the entrails of any bird or beast. He carried the carcass back to the clearing outside the city and there, on a flat stone, gutted and dismembered it. In all its outer parts, feathers, skin, eyes, talons, it was like a bird. Inside were bulging strands, some dun color, some yellowish, that were flexible and soft to the touch but so resistant that his Yen-metal sword could barely cut them; here were networks and skeins of red threads and blue; here clusters of white balls.

"Box, what sort of bird is this?"

"It is not any sort of bird. It is an engine."

Thorinn fingered a skein of blue threads. "I thought engines were made of metal, or wood."

"Engines can be made of anything, even flesh."

Thorinn absorbed this in silence; the box had told him so many fantastic things that he no longer thought it worthwhile to argue with it; but at length he said:

"Well, why would anybody want to make an engine that looks like a bird?"

"Perhaps to watch over you, Thorinn."

Thorinn dug a hole slowly with his sword, dropped the bird in and kicked dirt over it until the last dusty feather vanished. If the bird had been set to watch him by other engines, what would happen now that he had killed it?

He climbed to his tower room by leaping from one outside balcony to another, a quicker and more direct route than going up the well inside. He ate a chunk of dried meat and drank from the magic jug, then stretched himself on the floor with his hands over his head. Close to his ears there was a muted scrabbling and scratching, the sounds of the insects that lived on the false floor beneath the woven cords. He glimpsed them sometimes, gray and brown beetles, long colorless wrigglers.

His eye fell on the wooden pole that spanned the peak of the roof over his head. These poles were everywhere in the city; they must be perches for birds that preyed on the insects. As for the people of the city, Thorinn imagined them as winged too—tall men with dazzling white feathers like an eagle's, women soft as doves.

Perhaps he drowsed; at any rate, he came to himself with a start. Under him the floor vibrated in a short, sharp jolt; a distant sound came up the well below.

Thorinn leaped up, saved himself from floating away by grasping the floor cords with one hand, then with his toes. In a moment he had slung his belongings over his shoulders, and in another he was out the window and into a tree.

He clung to the branch and listened. At first he heard nothing unusual. A waterfowl squawked somewhere; then there was a faint, distant bawling. These sounds and others grew in a few moments to a babble of voices; Thorinn had never heard anything like it.

The wooded area around him was deserted; from where he was, he could not see into the courtyard or the fields beyond. He leaped back to the roof of the tower he had just left; clinging to the smooth bark, he thrust his head over and looked down.

Below him, the courtyard was full of dust and confusion. Broad pink and gray backs of beasts, small as beetles from this height, plunged toward the exit from the courtyard; there were dozens of them, no, hundreds, and beside them, flapping along close to the ground, were gray birds; they were goading the animals along with sticks held somehow beneath them. Now here came a sudden explosion of fowl, all nodding heads and yellow feet, and then after that a cluster of white animals with curved horns, all driven by the gray flapping creatures; they all passed out between the towers, and still more came from one of the ground-floor exits.

Thorinn could bear no more; he turned and slid down the roof head-foremost, leaned in, grasped the windowframe, pulled himself inside. The only other exit was a hole in the floor through which he passed into another empty room, and so on until he reached the top of the larger tower below. Here he leaned over the low railing of a balcony and peered down into the hall. It was dark and silent. He swung himself over and dropped from one balcony to another, pausing often to listen, until he had reached the floor two hundred ells down. Skylight, entering through the broad courtyard doorway, was full of yellow dust-motes. Thorinn leaped to the wall at one side of the entrance and cautiously put his head out. In the courtyard, fat grunting beasts and squawking fowl were being herded by flapping gray things—not birds, but men and women with wings like those of wingmice. They were shorter than he, with broad chests and bandy legs. Their long arms ended in three-fingered hands; their wings, which were like gray cloaks when they were folded, became taut membranes when they flew.

The sticks they used to goad the animals were clutched in their long toes.

Thorinn withdrew into the darkness and said in a low voice, "Box, are they men or demons?"

"Some are beasts and some are fowl."

"I mean the ones with the gray wings."

"They are engines, Thorinn."

"Engines too—like the bird? Wait a minute." The sounds outside had changed; there were squawkings, screeches, the flapping of wings. Bursting with curiosity, Thorinn put his head out again, and found himself staring straight into the face of a wingman who was pursuing half a dozen ducks escaped from the flock. The wingman's gray-furred face did not change; his dull eyes passed over Thorinn expressionlessly, and in a moment he was pursuing his ducks in the other direction.

After a moment Thorinn stepped out into the doorway, exposing himself fully. No one paid the slightest attention to him, even when he began moving across the courtyard toward the doorway from which the beasts and fowl were still issuing. The herdsmen's bodies were covered with short gray fur; their skin was a darker gray, their eyes brown. Their nails, on both hands and feet, were curved and horny. They wore tunics, kirtles, and caps of knitted wool, some plain, others with vivid designs in red, ocher, and blue. Between their thighs was a gray membrane anchored by a short tail, and all their garments were made with slits to accommodate the tail and wings.

As Thorinn drew near the doorway, a last explosion of ducks and other fowl burst out of it, followed by two wingmen; now he could see the floor of the central well inside, and he hopped in that direction, thinking the procession was over; but another wingman appeared, then four more, then another four, leaping up in the dimness out of what Thorinn now perceived was a huge oblong hole in the floor, with a lid tilted above it. Some sprang toward the outer doorway and were gone; others went flapping upward. The great well was murmurous with their wings, but otherwise they made no sound.

Thorinn knelt beside the opening and put his head down. For a moment he could not understand what he saw. On the floor of the chamber below, several ells back from the opening, were stacked bundles of silvery translucent material like those he had seen in the treasure cave. Wingmen were pulling these off the stacks, setting them upright, and then doing something to them which he could not make out, whereupon the silvery film vanished like water and another wingman sprang forth out of each. Wide as it was, the chamber was packed full of these bundles. The chamber itself was walled and floored with some glassy yellow-gray material that looked slippery but was not; the lid, which was held open at an angle in some way that Thorinn could not make out, was covered with the same stuff underneath but was packed dirt on the upper side.

The stacks were dwindling visibly, but still there was no end to them. To pass the time, Thorinn began counting the wingmen as they were revived; he got to five hundred and still they came; he had never imagined that there could be so many people in one place.

Now something new was happening. The wingmen and women as they were revived were not leaping to the exit but standing in a cluster as if waiting for something. Now he saw them stoop, and here came three or four of them in a line, each carrying a small bundle with exaggerated care. When they came near enough, he saw that each bundle was a child, sleeping or dead. They were perfect miniatures of the wingmen, with tiny gray-furred faces and closed eyelids as delicate as the ears of mice. Each was wrapped in a sort of pouch, with only its head exposed; the pouches were woven in bright geometric patterns. Each wingman leaped up out of the underground chamber with his burden, then grasped it with his toes, spread his wings, and went flapping up into the darkness.

"Box," said Thorinn in a whisper, "why are all the children asleep?"

"If the children were awake, they would know they are being brought into the cavern from another place."

"Well, and why not?"

"Then they would know there is another place when they grow up, and they might try to leave the cavern."

"But why not real men instead of engines? Or why not engines instead of children? It doesn't make any sense."

"There must be real children or it would make no sense to have engines which look like men. But there cannot be real men because they would remember another place. The children are too young to remember. When they are grown they will take the engines' place and will think men have always lived here."

Thorinn tried half-heartedly to puzzle this out, but his attention was distracted: the chamber was emptying rapidly. The last stacks were being taken down, and behind them he could see the rear wall of the chamber, but there was no sign of a tunnel opening yet. He waited with increasing impatience while the few remaining stacks were dismantled, denying to himself what he saw: the rear wall was unbroken.

"Thorinn, there is a danger to you unless you leave this place quickly."

He turned and saw the last few wingmen crowding out through the opening. He followed them; they did something to the lid and it slowly descended, closing the chamber.

"Box," he said, "where is the tunnel?"

"There is no tunnel, Thorinn."

He had known it, he supposed, all the time.

While he was asleep they had all gone into the underground chamber to hide, and had set the bird to watch him. He would have lived out his life here, and then the bird would have told them he was dead (or rather, it would have stopped telling them he was alive), and they would have come out, just as they were doing now, to resume their existence—as if he had never been.

11

How Thorinn tried to fly without success, and built a bladder instead.

The fields around the city were full of wingmen, and so were the byres, orchards, sheds, and the towers themselves. Wingmen and women were everywhere, setting things to rights, cleaning, repairing, weeding, gardening. The towers were aswarm with them; the sound of their wings, many times multiplied, made a susurant whispering. Thorinn put his head into a few of the rooms on the lowest level and found joiners joining, tailors sewing, weavers weaving. None of them acknowledged his existence by so much as a glance or gesture.

He climbed the well to the upper rooms, buffeted by the wind of wings that missed him by finger-spans, and searched until he found some of the children asleep in hammocks of woven cord. Their small faces were serene. "When will they wake up?" he asked the box.

"When all the signs that they come from another place are gone."

"But they did come from another place—they'll remember that, won't they?"

"The other place is just like this place."

"How do you know all that?"

"I don't know it, Thorinn, but it must be so, or all this would
be senseless."

The wingmen toiled by day and night; they never slept, and
even when the sky was so overcast that Thorinn could not see his
hand before his face, they seemed to need no artificial light. When
Thorinn approached them out of curiosity, aiming his light-box at
their faces, they turned as if half asleep, blinked at his light, then
went back to their labors.

Thorinn had made himself a shelter in the grove near the town,
disliking the idea of sleeping under the wingmen's roof, although
he well knew that they could find him anywhere if they meant him
harm. On the third morning, when he poked his nose into the pan-
tries for something to eat, he heard the piping of tiny voices
above: the children were awake.

He found them here and there, some at their lessons, some in a
nursery, some following the wingmen and women about at their
daily tasks. Unlike the wingmen, the children stared at Thorinn
with frank curiosity. One of them tugged at a woman's garments
and said something; the woman answered curtly and drew the
child away.

"What were they saying, box?"

"I think the child was saying, 'Who is that person?' and the engine was saying, 'Never mind.' There is danger for you, Thorinn, if
the engines believe you might harm the children."

"I, harm the children?" said Thorinn indignantly. Indeed, there
was something about them that drew him: they were like the
young of rabbits or mice, innocent, tender, and beautiful. Now
that he saw them beside the wingmen and women, he could well
believe that the adults were engines, and he wondered that he had
not seen it before. The big wingmen had dull faces; they were like
the bark-creatures animated by Snorri in the tale; the children
were bright-eyed, full of life.

Now that the children were awake, the adults no longer worked
day and night; they slept, or appeared to sleep, hanging head
downward from the perches in their apartments. Cooks were busy
in the kitchens where, instead of fireplaces or ovens, they had
great heaps of rotted vegetable matter secured in wooden presses;

and the heat from these, as Thorinn felt for himself by putting his hand near them, was sufficient to cook their food.

The children were of different sizes, the smallest so young that they were just beginning to learn to fly, the biggest perhaps four summers older. They followed Thorinn about, in spite of the attempts of the wingmen to prevent it, and two or three turned up so often that Thorinn learned to watch for their faces. The box spoke to them whenever there was opportunity, and after a few days it could tell Thorinn what they said.

"Where do you come from?" was their persistent question. Thorinn told the box to answer that he came from the sky, but this did not satisfy them. Once when he was prowling along the wall of the cavern west of the city, followed as usual by two children whom he called Sven and Ilge (their own names were unpronounceable), the children stopped him and pointed to a cleft in the rock, no wider than two fingers' breadth. "Here is where you come from," they told him.

"What, from that little hole?"

"It is too small now, but you were smaller before."

"I don't know what you mean. When was I smaller?"

"When you came out of the rock." Sven thrust his fingers into the cleft and pulled them out again, drawing his small hands apart as if to indicate something that emerged and grew. After a few more questions and replies it became clear that he thought Thorinn had really come out of the stone itself. "Like sap dripping from a tree?"

The child's face was merry. "Yes, just like that. Naturally you do not remember; you had just come into the Egg."

"No, that was not what happened."

"Then," said Ilge, "how did you get into the Egg?"

Thorinn hesitated, thinking of the cataract which could be seen in the distance from where they stood, but some obscure instinct made him lie. "From another crack," he said.

He walked on, with the children fluttering about him. "But not a crack like that," he said. "A big one, a tunnel, like this." He held his arms out. The box seemed to be having trouble; it spoke, Sven answered, it spoke again. Ilge looked puzzled. She repeated Thorinn's gesture: "Like this? A crack? Where is there such a crack in the Egg?"

"Well, it is hidden."

Sven sniggered. "It must be well hidden."

"Someday I may show you."

"And in such a crack, there could be three Thorinns and not one."

"Oh, yes, and not three but hundreds."

"Hundreds!" Both children doubled over with helpless laughter, and fell into a leafy bush.

One morning he found the older children sitting in rows in a large room where a wingman in a yellow gown was making them repeat after him sentences which he read out from a book of reeds. Thorinn sat down and let the box tell him what they were saying; it seemed to be a fanciful account of the creation of the world. Presently he noticed that the wingman was speaking briefly, but the box at some length.

"Box, why is everything so much shorter when he says it?"

"In their language there are words which contain the meaning of several words together."

"How can that be? Tell me what he is really saying now."

"He is saying, 'Shéshiru fállana állishi hóloshen—' "

"No, I don't mean that, I mean what are the words that have several words in them?"

"Just now, when he talked about the shell of the Egg, he said, 'Shéshiru,' which means something that lasts a long time; then 'fállana,' meaning early life, then 'állishi,' meaning that time is what the sentence is about; then 'hóloshen,' of years; then 'shiri-shirishíri,' meaning dozens of dozens of dozens; then 'lun,' which means nine, then 'leshíren,' not yet—"

"But that's nothing like what you said before," Thorinn protested. "It doesn't even make sense. How can they understand each other?"

He forgot to listen to the box's reply, for the children were standing up, bowing to the yellow-gowned man, then marching out the door, glancing at Thorinn out of the corners of their eyes. He heard them take wing a few moments later, fluttering up and down the well.

He still had no idea how he could get through the cataract, even supposing he could reach it; but the first thing was to find a way of getting there. If the wingpeople could fly with their leathery wings, why not he? In one of the workshops he found two pieces of tanned leather, supple and thin, each more than an ell wide and long. He spread them out on a table and cut them into triangles, each with thongs at intervals—a waste of good leather, but it saved him the trouble of attaching separate thongs to them later. He had contrived the triangular pieces so that he could attach them to his arms at wrist, elbow and shoulder, and to his legs at hip and knee; in this way, he thought, he could improve on the design of the real wings, which extended only to the waist, and make up for the lack of the tail and the leathery flap that went with it.

Standing in a meadow near the city, with an interested audience of children, he leaned forward slightly, raised his arms and lowered them with a strong movement. He felt a surge that lifted him off the ground. Encouraged, he repeated the movement again and again; he felt himself being propelled upward, but the world was tilting; he strove in vain to right himself; now he was looking directly upward at the sky, and now the ground smote him on the back.

After several more attempts, each ending in the same way, to the vast entertainment of the children, he concluded that there must be some reason for the wingmen's tails, although he could not see what it was, and he gave up the idea of flying.

Spring was now well advanced, the crops growing in the fields, the orchard trees in blossom, scenting the air with a powdery piercing sweetness. Drifts of petals rose into the sky when the wind blew. On five successive mornings the wingpeople stood outside the town to watch them; they sang and played music on bone flutes, then swarmed back into the towers.

Several times more he saw the river whipped by the wind into slender waves taller than a man, and he never ceased to marvel that so light a breeze could make the waves so tall. In a way he understood the symmetry of it, that because the water weighed so little the strength of the wind against it was greater: but what if the water weighed nothing at all—how high would the waves be then?

Caged and restless, he spent days wandering in the forest, searching the cliff wall for crevices, staring at the cataract. Somehow he must find his way through it—but then what? He was already too many thousands of leagues from the Midworld to hope ever to get back afoot. The moment he came to any shaft, the geas

would force him to go down. It was frustrating to know that he
had killed demons and survived many perils, and yet he could not
escape the power of that one old man up in Hovenskar. Sometimes he thought he felt Goryat's eyes on him wherever he went:
or perhaps not Goryat, but someone even more powerful, some
old god crouching at the center of things, with his hands and eyes
everywhere.

What if he gave himself no choice but to go up when he came
to a shaft? If some engine were to carry him up as irresistibly as
an engine had carried him down. . . .

He came back to the thought of the engine the box had shown
him, the bladder filled with a gas lighter than air, a basket suspended beneath it, himself in the basket, rising. . . . Clouds were
lighter than the air, else they would fall, and so was the smoke
from a fire. The bladder could be held open above a fire so that
the smoke went in; thus it would rise, but then how to make it
come down again? In the normal course of things smoke never
came down. Perhaps a hole could be pierced in the top of the
bladder, with a cover over it; remove the cover, the smoke es-
capes, the bladder descends.

One morning, surrounded by children as usual, he experimented
with a bladder taken from the body of a horned forest animal he
had killed the day before. The children watched in fascination as
he kindled a fire of twigs, then set to work scraping the bladder
clean, drying it, and tying off one end with a bit of cord. He
spread the other end open with two crossed twigs and held it
above the little fire.

"They want to know what you are doing now," the box said.

"Tell them I want to see if the smoke will make the bladder
rise."

The box spoke with them briefly and then said, "They say they
will make it rise for you if you like."

"Tell them to be quiet." The bladder was growing plump in
Thorinn's hands; it trembled, moved; he released it and it ascended
slowly an ell or two over his head before it gently capsized in the
air and came down again. The children were fluttering around
in their excitement, ignoring the light drizzle that had begun to fall.
One came to him and grasped his hand earnestly, speaking into his
face. "What is she saying?" he asked.

"She is saying that you are a magician, the greatest in the Egg. She asks that you bring her pet bird back to life."

"Tell her I know no such magic."

The box spoke; the child, with a sulky face, moved away. Thorinn was looking at the limp bladder. Evidently what it needed was a weight to keep it upright, so that the smoke could not spill out and be lost. After some thought he bent a twig into a circlet and tied it securely with cord; this served to weigh down the bottom of the bladder as well as to hold the mouth of it open.

This time he used a smaller fire and held the bladder closer. The bladder filled very satisfactorily with smoke and rose a dozen ells in the air, to Thorinn's delight and the awe of the children; but after a few minutes it took on a wrinkled appearance, sagged, and began to descend. When he picked it up it was flabby; nearly all the smoke had escaped.

He tried again, and this time tied a cord tightly around the neck of the bladder above the ring as soon as it was filled; the bladder rose as before and stayed up much longer, but it came down again just the same. The children were as disappointed as he was.

He examined the bladder carefully for holes and found none; it must be that the smoke was escaping through the tied-off portion at the top, and perhaps through the bottom as well. This was a disappointment; if the smoke could not be kept in the bladder longer than that, the larger version he had in mind would be of no use even to escape from the cavern, let alone to get back to the Midworld.

He untied the neck of the bladder and looked at it glumly. The inside of it was moist to the touch, although it had been dry before: had the smoke turned to water when it cooled? Then all the children wanted to feel the bladder too. One of them tugged at his arm and spoke earnestly.

"He says the fire should be attached to the bladder, then the bladder will keep going up," said the box.

Thorinn opened his mouth, then closed it again. With a charred twig he sketched on the side of a stone, while the children clustered around to watch: here the bladder, here the ring to hold the neck open, and here, suspended from the ring, a basket for the rider. Now, inside the basket, a fire pot lined with clay or earth: the fire ascends with the bladder, and as long as it burns the smoke cannot cool and turn to water; therefore the bladder stays

aloft. But the basket can carry only so much wood to burn; when
that is gone, down comes the bladder.

Thorinn fed more twigs to the fire to keep it from going out in
the light drizzle. The air shimmered over the embers; flakes of
white ash rose, wavered, and fell, yet there was no wind. Thorinn
struggled with a thought: suppose it was not the smoke at all, but
the air heated by the fire, that made the bladder rise?

At all events, he must begin to plan now for a bladder big
enough to carry him and his possessions: how big must it be? The
box was of no use: "That depends on the weight of the bladder
and the lifting power of the air." When Thorinn asked what the
lifting power of air was, the box replied, "That depends on how
hot it is, and how hot the air around the bladder is."

"How am I to find that out?"

The box showed him a picture of a slender rod of glass, with
marks on it and a thread of silver inside. "This is an engine for
measuring how hot a thing is."

"But where am I to get such an engine?"

"I don't know, Thorinn."

So it was evident that he must do it himself, and in truth he was
rather glad of that, for when he asked the box's advice it always
told him more than he wanted to know and more than he could
understand, whereas when he worked a thing out for himself, no
matter how difficult it was, at least when he was done he understood it.

That afternoon he made weights by cutting a stick into little
pieces of equal length, and by attaching one after another to the
neck of the bladder, determined how much it could lift when it
was filled with hot air. He also found out by accident that he
could measure equally well and much more easily by attaching a
long cord to the bladder: then it rose until the lifting power of the
air inside it exactly matched the weight of the cord which it raised
from the ground.

From these studies Thorinn concluded that the height of the
bladder ought to be at least eight times his own height in order to
bear him and his belongings aloft. That meant a bladder sixteen or
seventeen ells tall, much bigger than he had imagined it would be.
He was tempted to make it smaller and therefore easier, but if it
did not raise him, the work would be all for nothing.

Because the bladder must bear its own weight as well as his, he wanted to make it as light as possible, and for this reason he gave up his first intention of making it out of pieces of leather or cloth; instead, he pieced it together out of the thin, parchment-like stuff the wingpeople used for interior walls and screens. Aided by Sven and Ilge, he cleared a space in one of the largest workshops and took what he needed. Presently the wingpeople brought more wall-stuff to replace what he had taken; when he needed more, he took that as well.

One morning he came upon Sven and Ilge in the workshop trying clumsily to fit a whittled stick into the hollow of a reed. Between amusement and sympathy, Thorinn explained to them through the box that both shaft and plunger must be perfectly round, or the fire stick would not work. Their grey-furred little faces were so earnest and trusting that he could not leave it at that, although he was impatient to get on with his own task. He found a good rod of hardwood in the wingmen's stores, for a plunger, and showed them how the shaft must be made in two halves carved to fit around it, then slowly tightened as the plunger was turned between them with wet sand to grind the pieces to a perfect fit, and finally glued together with an end-piece shaped to leave a hollow for the tinder. He left them toiling earnestly and clumsily at the task; he doubted that they could accomplish it, but at least they were happy in trying.

He made his bladder in six sections shaped like a fish, each twenty ells long and nine ells wide. Under his direction, the children joined the pieces that made up each section with fish-glue, and hung the sections up to dry in the well. When that was done, Thorinn brought the sections back into his workroom, which in the meantime the wingpeople had begun to use again for their own purposes: he cleared out their benches, jars, and other rubbish, spread the sections on the floor, and began gluing the edges together. It proved exasperatingly difficult to make the flat pieces form a round shape without wrinkling or buckling, but after many failures he got the whole bladder assembled. He painted it all over with fish-glue, dried it again, and at last carried it outside for trial. Children trooped out after him.

It was a still gray day. Thorinn unfolded his bladder and hung it from a cord stretched between two trees, with the neck about three ells from the ground. He made a ring of a bent sapling and secured it inside the neck. Beneath it he laid dry brush and branches in criss-cross layers, and kindled a fire. Flames curled up; smoke poured into the open neck of the bladder, and presently it began to fill. To Thorinn's disgust, a moment later there came a patter of raindrops in the trees and on the suspended limp bulk of the bladder. A gust of wind blew sparks slanting away from the fire; then the patter increased to a stuttering roar; water swept across the clearing in veils and torrents. Thorinn retreated to shelter until the rain stopped; by that time the fire was out.

Thorinn sent the children for dry wood. They found it without delay; the ground was dry only a few hundred ells distant. Thorinn built another fire and lighted it. After about the same interval, it rained again and put the fire out.

Thorinn saw then that whoever ruled the world, whether it was gods, demons, or even engines as the box seemed to think, they did not want him to inflate his bladder today. But he was loath to take it down, dry it and fold it, and put it away indoors, only to take it out again tomorrow.

What if there were a roof over the bladder and the fire, to keep the rain off while the bladder filled? Such a roof would take him the rest of the day to build, and then it would be in the way when the bladder rose. . . . But why not use the bladder itself as a roof?

He cut a pole a little less than three times his height, measured the bladder with it, cut it again, and used it as a measure to cut another the same length. He trimmed and whittled the ends carefully to roundness, so that they should not puncture the bladder. Leaping up with the first pole through the open neck, he managed to get it crosswise at an angle; then hanging from it and pulling the fabric of the bladder down, he adjusted it until it was level. He did the same with the second pole, crosswise to the first. Now the bladder was spread at four points to its full width of about seventeen ells, although it was hollow between. Thorinn built a third fire.

As he had more than half expected, it rained again. Now the spread bulk of the bladder sheltered the fire, although the rain smoked and streamed all around it. The hollow places between the poles began to fill out; watching from his place under the tree, Thorinn thought he saw the bladder straining upward. Exultantly, he took a step forward. While he was still in midair, there came a shattering crack and a white glare. Thorinn tumbled into the un-

derbrush, blinded, stunned, and deaf. When he picked himself up
again, the children's cries were receding in the distance and the
bladder was in flames. Yellowish smoke was pouring from the fire;
presently it went out. The rain continued, turning the fire into a
soggy pile of ash. What was left of the bladder hung by its cord
from a single tree; the other was split and slivered at the base, as
if it had been struck by a mighty hammer; bits of the white wood
lay scattered all over the clearing.

Thorinn sat looking at the ruins of his work. He felt a sudden
elation, and realized after a moment what it was about: he knew a
way to get up through the cataract.

"Box, if it should rain here so long that the valley is flooded,
will the waterfall keep on flowing or will it stop?"

"It will stop, Thorinn."

So it must be; the rulers of the world, whoever they were, could
not be expected to take such care of their subjects, only to let
them drown in a flooded cavern. Now his way was clear.

Only two panels of the bladder had been ruined by the light-
ning, which had run down them like a crooked river, burning
away a channel nearly a span in width and leaving the edges
blackened. Thorinn made new panels, fitted them into place, glued
and dried them.

In one of the workshops he found a basket adequate for his
needs: it was round, nearly two ells broad, and two spans deep.
For a firepit he brought clay from the river bank and formed it like
a deep dish in the center of the basket, leaving a space half an ell
broad all around for himself and his possessions, including the
firewood and kindling he must take with him. The basket had four
handles by which he meant to suspend it; for this purpose he knotted together a rigging to fit over the inflated bladder. He attached
a long cord to the top of this rigging, and eight shorter ones at the
bottom which he brought together and fastened to the four handles of the basket. He also cut some pieces of wall-stuff to use as
patches in case the bladder was damaged.

Now he had to consider how to defend himself if he should be
attacked by an engine in the tunnels. He filled bags of flimsy paper
with pitch and bound them to the tips of the stoutest arrows he
could find. The bags burst and splattered when they struck a target, but he was not yet satisfied. What he wanted was something to

entangle the limbs of the engine. He thought of sticky cords bursting out of the bag—but if they were sticky, what was to keep them from clinging together?

He began again, using fishing lines which he coated with pitch and then coiled inside the bag. But the bursting of the bag did not carry them far; something else was needed. He thought of springs, and began to make small circlets of sapling branches, tied together with the thinnest thread. He fastened stone weights to the ends of his fishing lines and coiled them so that the weights lay against the ends of the circlets where they were joined. After many trials he discovered how to mix the pitch with just enough water and fish-glue to make the lines fly apart when the thread broke. In the end he had in each bag a complicated construction of three sapling-rings, each with its coiled and weighted cord, each set in a different direction. When he fired it at a tree, the sticky lines whipped out in all directions and tangled themselves among the branches.

He prepared ten of these pitch-arrows, and in addition took a quiverful of the ordinary kind.

Now he was almost ready. "Box," he said, "show me what way the engine brought me down into the cavern."

In the crystal appeared the outlines of a slanting tunnel. It forked, and one passage went steeply up while the other continued at the same pitch for a little space before it turned upward and became a vertical shaft. A tiny dot descended this shaft, moved down the slanting tunnel, and disappeared.

"Show me where the water runs."

The first fork and the stem of the Y filled with shimmering blue. "And that second shaft?" Thorinn asked, pointing. "Where does it go?"

The outlines drifted downward in the crystal. The shaft rose through a vast space and continued upward. At the far end of this space there were other shafts.

"What is that, another cavern like this one?"

"It is a cavern smaller than this one, and it is different in other ways."

"Are there men in it?"

"No, only engines."

Thorinn frowned. "Show me these engines."

In the crystal, he was looking into a cavern full of confusing shapes. An engine drifted by, then another. They paused, touched the side of one of the huge shapes that rose around them, then went on, for all the world like bees gathering pollen. They did not look at all like the engine that had captured him before. "Box, will they harm me?"

"No, Thorinn."

"And that shaft in the ceiling, where does it go?"

The view traveled upward, the lines shrank together, and he was looking at another maze of passages, shafts, and tunnels. "Will it take me back to the Midworld?"

"Yes."

How much of this could he believe? The conviction had been growing on him that the box was not to be trusted, and that if it had another chance to betray him it would do so. Well, he would see.

Early the next morning, before the children were awake, he collected all his belongings, including the tightly wrapped bladder with its basket, and set out for the upper end of the cavern. He built himself a little shelter of branches near the cavern wall, within sight and sound of the cataract, and lay there that night. On the following day he began cutting poles for a shed ten ells long, eight high, and four wide. He planted the poles on rising ground above the river, and lashed other poles to them to make a peaked roof. He thatched the roof with bundles of branches to the thickness of half an ell.

In the middle of the space covered by the shed he dug a firepit, and on either side he stacked dry wood from the forest. Then with his sword he cut through the trunks of four trees, forming a rough oblong around the shed, at a height of fifteen ells. He notched the stumps and cut the logs into pieces six ells long, which he raised with much toil, using a rope and a tripod of poles, and set into place at the ends of the oblong; he notched these in turn, and now cut more logs fourteen ells long, which he laid across the structure to form a solid flat roof above the peaked roof of the shed; and with leather thongs filched from the wingmen's workshops, he lashed the whole structure firmly together. All through this work, which occupied him fourteen days, the air was cloudless.

On the fifteenth day he built a fire in the pit and touched it off. The flames mounted; smoke poured up under the roof, and

Thorinn retreated to the shelter of a nearby tree. Presently the rain began; first a patter, then a steady hammering in the leaves above. Thorinn shut his eyes and waited. There was an earsplitting crack and a white glare that he could see through his eyelids. When he looked, he saw that the log roof above the shed was splintered but unbroken. The rain continued in a steady torrent. After a time, without warning, there was another lightning-stroke and a clap of thunder; again the roof was splintered—he could see the white spears standing up at all angles above it—but it held. The thatched roof beneath was not even touched.

Thorinn watched until the rain began to spatter from the overloaded leaves of the tree above him. He ran to the shed, stayed there long enough to bank his fire, and ran back drenched to his shelter near the cliff.

All day long the rain continued, and at intervals peals of thunder rolled down the valley and the sky was lighted with a violet glare. Toward evening Thorinn pulled his shirt over his head for a cloak and went down to the river. It was swollen and white-capped, twice as wide as before. He went back to the shelter, ate his evening meal, and fell asleep to the drumming of rain in the treetops.

Sometime during the night he woke up realizing that the sound had stopped. He ran to the shed and found that the fire had gone out, although the shed was intact and dry. He built the fire up again, waited as before until it was burning well, then banked it, and went back to bed. In the morning the river was a surging brown flood. Thorinn ventured out to the shed, found the fire low, and built it up once more. The log roof was a mass of splinters from the repeated lightning-strokes, but the splinters themselves, as he had hoped, made a roof almost as good for his purpose as the original.

The river sprawled wider, creeping almost visibly up the slope; by now, Thorinn thought, it must be almost to the wingmen's towers.

His stacks of wood were dwindling. Thorinn kept the fire going as charily as possible, and watched the river. On the following morning it was halfway up the slope; farther down he could see trees standing up out of it like marooned people. By now, surely, the water must be in the middle stories of the towers.

For the first time he began to doubt what he was doing. Would the invisible watchers really let the wingpeople's farms be flooded, their buildings swept away? He banked the fire again and went to bed, but it was long before he was asleep.

In the morning he awoke knowing that something had happened. He listened: the roar of the cataract had changed its note. He tumbled out and peered upward. Was the stream thinner, or was it his imagination? In a moment he was sure. A last white plume came majestically down the wall; above it he could see the dripping black hole in the stone.

Thorinn's instinct was for haste, but he made himself take the time to build up the fire again, then to assemble all his belongings into one compact bundle to be strapped on his back. He had decided against trying to inflate the bladder here and use it to reach the exit; in the first place, it would take too long, and second, he might drift up out of reach of the wall. Instead, he had brought with him a pot of pitch and two of the wingmen's brushes. Hanging the pot from his belt, he dipped one of the brushes now, slapped it against the stone, and pulled himself upward. As the sluggish weight of his bundle was drawn into motion, his task became easier; he tugged one brush free, dipped the other, and slapped it against the stone above his head.

He angled toward the hole in the wall as he went; he could see the interior now, still glistening with moisture, and a few thready streams of water that fell over the lip to join the drifting raindrops. The ground dropped away below him, blurred by rain. Here was the hole above him; he hauled himself up, grasped the lip and pulled himself over.

He sat up, gasping and triumphant. He was in a slanting tunnel twenty ells high, with rounded walls worn smooth by water.

12

How Thorinn battled flying engines in their cavern, and solved a riddle wrongly.

Down the middle of the passage ran a steady trickle of water where a torrent had run before. The darkness was broken only by his light-box and the silence by the murmur of water. He scanned the ceiling eagerly as he went, but it was unbroken, league after league. His good leg grew tired, and he stopped to rest and massage it. He drank from the little stream; like the river below, it had the taste of the stone in it. Then he went on. It seemed to him that the day must be almost over, below in the cavern. How long would his fire burn, and how long after that would the water begin to recede?

An engine had brought him into the cavern through the water, but he was no fish; if the water flowed here again before he found some exit, he must drown.

The bulk of his belongings, light as it was, strained at his shoulders with each leap, like a hand pulling him insistently back. At first, indeed, he had thought it was the geas, but it seemed that the voice in his head understood that there was no way to go down from the cavern, and it was silent.

If only he could inflate the bladder, it would be easier to get up this steep tunnel, but he dared not pause long enough to do so, and even if he did, the bladder would hide the exit from him and he might never see it.

Presently the stream diminished but became more agitated— great slow swells were traveling down the tunnel at his feet, and up ahead he could see that the swells were higher and sharper. Now he could hear the melancholy sound of falling water, and now he could see it: thin sheets dropping from the ceiling far overhead, striking the tunnel floor and rebounding in slow fantastic shapes. The opening above appeared to be circular and as wide as the tunnel itself, but it was hard to tell because the air was full of streamers and floating droplets of water.

The water dripped like syrup from the opening above, fell and struck with dreamlike slowness, splattered the walls, ran down black and glistening. Thorinn leaped through, landed beyond where the tunnel was almost dry. Ahead, the tunnel continued at the same slope for another fifty ells and then curved majestically upward. Thorinn peered up, shielding the light-box with his hand: the tunnel, now a shaft, was straight, smooth-walled and dry, as far upward as he could see.

Thorinn unwrapped his bundle and spread it out on the stone floor. He uncovered his pitch pot and brushes, tied the light-box to his arm, took the end of the cord attached to the top of the bladder, and leaped upward. Clinging by a tarry brush, he pulled the limp bladder toward him until he thought it was high enough, then dipped a section of the cord in the pot and secured it to the wall. He leaped down again, and found that the bladder was still too low: the neck of it was almost touching the basket. He measured the slack with his arm, then went up again, hauled up more cord, and secured it as before.

Now the bladder was hanging properly at the bend of the tunnel where it turned upward and became a shaft. Thorinn loaded all his possessions into the space between the firepit and the wall of the basket, kindled a fire, added bits of wood, then larger pieces. The smoke rose through the open neck of the bladder; slowly it began to fill.

At first the bladder hung straight; then as it fattened, the tether on the wall above forced it to tilt outward more and more. Presently the neck of the bladder was no longer directly above the fire;

much smoke was being lost. Thorinn leaned against the basket, forced it upward on the slope, but now the basket tilted, and it was all he could do to hold it level so that the fire should not spill out and ignite the basket.

As he stood there, leaning with all his strength against the basket and craning his neck to see how the bladder was filling, a sudden clatter came from the tunnel below him. He turned, losing his hold on the basket, and saw with horror a great silvery sheet of water descending into the tunnel. The clatter became a roar; waves nearly as tall as the ceiling began to surge toward him; he was drenched by flying droplets where he stood. Desperately Thorinn turned and lifted the basket again.

Water was leaping and frothing around his ankles, and still the roar of the cataract swelled until he was half deafened. There was a faint tug at the basket, and the neck of the bladder above him tilted back a little; the bladder was rising.

Another tug, and the basket rose half a span, but when he tried to put his weight on it, down it swung again. The water was lapping at his knees. Up went the basket, another span or so. Thorinn's only thought was to shield the fire with his body.

Up it went again, Thorinn clinging to it; he raised his legs, and still the basket hung level. It crept upward once more, and this time went on rising. The water fell away below.

Thorinn clambered carefully into the basket, on the side across from his heaped possessions, and watched the smooth shaft move by. When the end of the cord came into view, he climbed the rigging of the bladder until he could catch the loop in his hand and tug it free of the wall. He climbed higher, almost to the widest part of the bladder, and thrust against the wall with his feet until the bladder reluctantly drifted away an ell or so; then he clambered back down into the basket, feeling weak and spent.

The walls of the shaft moved steadily and slowly past him. Below, the bottom was lost in darkness, and there was nothing but darkness above.

Lulled by the silence, Thorinn almost failed to notice when the movement of the walls slowed down. Hurriedly he built up the fire. The bladder hesitated, then bobbed upward, and its steady rise resumed.

In this dark shaft under the earth he had no sense of motion at all; it seemed rather that the shaft itself was in movement while he hung like a beetle on a string. The walls were smooth, gray, and featureless; there was nothing to mark off one place from another, and he began to feel that something had gone wrong with time; he could not tell how long he had been in the shaft.

He built up the fire again. His stock of fuel was dwindling. He opened one of his bundles, ate some cheese and drank from the jug. The box, which had been in the same bundle, lay on the floor of the basket at his feet.

"Box," he said, "how much farther is it to the cavern you showed me?"

"It is less than ten ells."

As the box spoke, Thorinn became aware of a red glow, like the glare from an oven at night but much dimmer and darker. Seized by fear, he was at the edge of the basket ready to leap out before he mastered himself. There was no heat in the steady red glare; he felt nothing when he held out his hand to it. "Box, why is it red?" he called.

"It is red because the engines see by red light."

Now, as the bladder rose, he could see the rim of the shaft, with unfamiliar tall shapes beyond it. He strung his bow, made sure the sheaf of arrows was lying ready to hand.

Now the lip of the shaft dropped away, and he saw that they were rising through a vast red-lit gulf in which a confusion of tall ovoid shapes rose one on another, with slender pedestals between them. Here and there were dots of brighter red, some so distant that they were like grains of dust. In the sullen gloom the walls and ceiling of the cavern were invisible; he could not rid himself of the conviction that he was in a great furnace, about to crisp and burst into flame. "Box, how high is this cavern?"

"It is seventy ells high."

"And the shaft goes straight through it?"

"Yes, Thorinn."

Now, as his eyes grew more accustomed to the dimness, he saw a distant movement through the aisles between the columns; a red eye winked on. It was coming closer. He reached for the box, turned it. "Box, what is that?"

"It is an engine."

"What sort of engine?"

"It is an engine that tends other engines."

Now he could see the spidery shape behind the light, looming nearer. Another red eye winked on in the distance, then another. The first engine was so near that he could see its skeletal arms outstretched, the sheen of something round and water-bright in its belly. He felt a sudden chill around his ankles, and looked down to see that the yellow flames of his fire had magically vanished. Even the embers were not alight; there was nothing but blackened wood and sullen red ash. Incredulous, he passed his hand over the charred sticks, then touched them. They were as cool as if the fire had gone out days ago.

"Box!" he cried.

"Here am I."

But he had no time for questions. The second and third engines were soaring past the bladder; the first had disappeared below. He felt a jolt, and the bladder dipped toward the nearest columns; another, and it moved again. He leaped to the other side of the basket, and saw that two engines were pushing the bladder above, half visible beyond its bulge. Another jolt, and a hiss; the bladder was moving, dropping. Thorinn leaned over the edge of the basket and saw the shaft below drifting away out of reach. "Box!"

"Here am I."

Feverishly Thorinn piled tinder and kindling under the dead fire, got out his fire stick, saw the yellow flames curl up. After a moment there was another wave of cold, and the flames vanished. He turned to see an engine soaring by, no more than two ells away.

Trembling with fear and anger, he seized an arrow, nocked it, let fly. He saw the arrow strike fair in the center of the engine, saw the pitch-smeared cords spring out and wrap themselves around it. He heard a shriek and a clatter; the engine drifted away aslant between the columns.

Another jolt came, and another. Thorinn nocked an arrow, fired at one of the engines above. He saw the pitch burst on the tail of the engine, but nothing more happened. The bladder was still drifting steadily downward away from the shaft; now it was passing between two columns of the tall shapes that stood one above another like gigantic beads on a wire. A hundred ells away, the forest ended and he glimpsed a broad open space with other shapes beyond it.

Thorinn slung his bow over his shoulder, seized two arrows and put them between his teeth. He sprang for the rigging, pulled himself up along the fat bulge.

Now he could see the two engines with their noses against the bladder, and the water-bright disks in their bellies. He jammed his foot under one of the cords of the rigging, forced his bow arm under another, and took aim at one of the engines. He struck it as he had the other, heard it shriek.

Slowly it tilted, came drifting down. In the dazzle of its red eye, he saw the spidery arms reaching for him, saw the round place in its belly no longer a bright disk but four curved blades like the petals of a flower, tangled and still. He drew his sword, struck at the reaching arm, heard a clang. The engine, slowly tumbling, passed on.

Thorinn put his sword away, nocked another arrow, and shot the third engine. It died in its turn, drifting downward, its spidery arms vainly reaching. In the silence, he heard the hiss of escaping air above.

He climbed higher to look, and found two long rents in the fabric; the bladder around them was crinkling, collapsing. Filled with fury, he climbed down to the basket again. He gave the box one burning glance, but did not speak to it. He tore open a bundle, found his patches, stuffed a handful of them into his belt. He dropped the bow, seized his pitch-pot and brush, and sprang up through the neck of the bladder.

In the stifling red dimness, he pulled himself up by grasping folds of the bladder, found the first hole. Gripping the handle of the pitch-pot between his teeth, he dipped his brush, painted the edges thickly, then got a patch from his belt and pressed it over the rent. He climbed higher, dealt with the other hole in the same way, then lowered himself again and dropped into the basket.

Below, one of the engines was drifting into the stem between two of the tall ovoids of a column. It struck with a distant clang, rebounded, slowly tumbled in the air, and resumed its gradual motion toward the floor of the cavern.

Thorinn lighted his fire again. The flames flickered up yellow, spread, caught. But the bladder had already passed through the metal forest and was slowly settling into the open space.

What was to be done now? The only way to get back to the shaft was to descend and go afoot, dragging the bladder after him. He separated the burning sticks a little; the bladder continued its gentle descent. At length the basket touched the floor, scraped a little, and was still.

Thorinn stepped out of the basket; relieved of his weight, it began to rise. Thorinn caught the trailing cord and felt its tug lift him almost but not quite off his feet. To be safe, he knotted the cord around his waist, but when he tried to walk, he found that his feet had no purchase on the floor; the most he could do was to hop straight upward, whereupon the bladder ponderously bobbed upward, too, then as gradually settled.

While he was puzzling over this, the shapes beyond him caught his eye. At a little distance there were four slender curving tracks of pinkish metal suspended high in the air; in the red gloom, they seemed to be aimed at two cavernous doorways in the wall beyond. Along the wall, past the metal tracks, he could make out lines of bulbous objects like metal eggs, as big as the bladder. As he watched, an egg detached itself from the row, was lifted to one of the tracks, and disappeared rapidly into a doorway. Presently another egg emerged from the other doorway in a cloud of steam, traveled along another track, and moved out of sight. Whatever these things were, they seemed to be paying no attention to him.

He turned away and stared out over the tops of the forest of columns. The best thing, perhaps, would be to build up his fire again, rise to the top of the cavern, then discharge one of his arrows at the ceiling with a cord tied to it. If the pitch held, he could draw the cord in and thus pull the bladder along; then pull the arrow free, shoot it again, and so on. . . . Out there, where the opening of the shaft must be, a tiny dot of red had winked into being. It drifted a little, then hung steady; but now he saw that it was growing brighter. It was coming toward him, and it was moving too fast to be one of the little engines he had slain.

Thorinn climbed hurriedly into the basket. "Box," he said bitterly, "what is that engine?"

"It is an engine like the one that took you prisoner before. There is a danger to you, Thorinn."

"So I see."

With grim haste, Thorinn was dipping the brush in the pitchpot, dabbing a spot the size of his fingernail onto the sole of each shoe. He unfastened the cord from about his waist, then slung the box over his shoulder, leaped out again and drifted toward the floor. "Where do those doorways go?" he demanded.

"One of them goes to a shaft where rising clouds carry things upward. The other goes to a shaft where falling water carries things down."

Thorinn's good foot touched the floor, clung. He strained forward, tugging the bladder after him. Another step, then another. The great awkward bulk of the bladder was in motion now, but it prevented him from looking back to see how close the engine was.

Lurching from good foot to bad, Thorinn tugged the bladder onward. Now he could see that there were spidery arms on the tracks, shaped to grip the metal eggs. While he watched, another dripping egg emerged from one of the doorways, traveled rapidly away, and was gone. It was no good asking the box which doorway was which, for he knew it would lie. Then he saw that was the answer.

"Box," he said, "which is the shaft that goes up?"

"It is the one on the left, Thorinn."

With a humorless grin, Thorinn leaped for the metal track on the right. The bladder bobbed up beside him. Clinging like a fly to the metal, Thorinn drew the bladder in. The red dot, now a disk, was shockingly near. He settled the bladder on the track between two spidery arms, saw them close to hold it, and tumbled into the basket as the track began to move, first slowly, then with such speed that the air whistled past his cheeks. Ahead, the doorway was blocked by a silvery pink film; it broke as the bladder entered it, and the air was suddenly full of flying droplets of spray. Bladder, basket, Thorinn and all were whirled out and downward into a chaos of roaring water.

Go down, said the voice triumphantly in his head.

13

How Thorinn died and was brought to life again, but resented it.

. . . it was therefore decided to put the Monitor on command mode with instructions to take whatever action may be necessary to promote the welfare of any remnant of humanity that may survive. No sono reports from the upper regions have come through since the fighting began. Nearly the whole of Lozed is flamed out and uninhabitable. If any of us live through the next few days, we will return and again put the Monitor on slave mode. If not, the destiny of mankind is in its—I had almost said hands. May God have mercy on us.

In the first instant the battering force of the water had collapsed the bladder around him. Suspended helplessly in the dark torrent, he had fought until he could hold his breath no longer; then as the water filled his lungs the crumpled bladder had turned somehow into the coils of a serpent that wound around his chest, constricting it with a pain beyond pain. The serpent was still there, although he could not see it when he opened his eyes. He struggled

uselessly. He was falling, but the curved wall of the room hung
steady around him. Some crystal thing was withdrawing over his
head. Metal tubes, arms, were moving away. The yellowish light
came from panels in the wall. A white engine drifted into view
from above; he could hear its faint hissing in the silence. White
spidery arms came out of it, turned, dipped, closed around him
gently at arms and thigh. He was too weak to resist. The arms re-
tracted, turned as the room wheeled around him, placed him with
his back against the long shaft of the engine that ended in a curved
tube over his head. Soft coils snaked around him. The hiss came
again, and he was moving upward through a round hole in the
ceiling. He came out into a room that was like a quarter of a
cheese, with one wall curved like the one below, the other two
straight; ceiling and floor were flat.

The coils withdrew; the arms gripped him again, turned him,
gently pressed him against a flattened pole that stood in the
corner. Other coils moved around him. The engine backed away
with a hiss, descended through the hole in the floor and was gone.
He was still falling, while the room fell around him. In a net bulging from the wall beside him he saw his possessions, the bundles,
the talking box, his shoes and clothing. He looked down at himself, saw that he was naked.

"Box," he said. His voice was thin and hoarse.

"Here am I."

"What is this place? What happened?"

"This is a place at the bottom of the world. You went into the
falling water and died. Engines brought you here."

"I'm alive," Thorinn muttered. "I didn't die."

"Engines made you live again." The box said something more,
but already Thorinn's eyes had closed and he was drifting away
into another dream of serpents.

When he awoke the second time he was still in pain, but he was
stronger. The unfamiliar room was just the same. "Box, I'm
thirsty," he said.

"There is water in the engine on the wall."

Thorinn looked, and saw two segmented yellow ropes that hung
outward like snakes from the white wall.

"One is for food, the other for water. The one on the right is
for water."

Thorinn reached, pulled the tube toward him, doubtfully put

the gray end of it between his lips. Cool sweet water spurted into his mouth; he choked with surprise, then swallowed. When he let go, the tube went back partway into the wall and was still. A few droplets of water, perfect little balls, drifted in the air.

There were glowing panels in the curved wall facing him, like the ones in the room below, and under them were six crystals like the one in the box, but much larger. Two were twice the size of the others; each of these had a smaller one on either side. In the middle of the room were two yellow poles, about an ell and a half apart, with large blue beads on them at intervals. To his left there was an upright box taller than a man, and beside it, in the corner, a half partition. Otherwise the room was empty. The air was pleasantly warm, but had an odd scent.

He examined the coils that were holding him, found that they were two fat white bands of some unfamiliar material, one under his armpits and the other across his thighs. He tried to pull them loose without success, until he discovered that they were clasped together on one side. He tugged at the ends and they came free. He was drifting away from the pole; the room was massively and slowly turning. He managed to seize the pole as it came around and drew himself to it, but his legs floated upward.

"Box," he said, "where are we going?"

"We are not going anywhere."

Thorinn clung to the pole with arms and legs; the room steadied a little. "I mean," he said with strained patience, "how long must we go on falling?"

"We are not falling. This place is at the bottom of the world." The crystal lighted, and he saw a dark circle with a dot of light at the center. Yellow lines appeared, radiating from the center. "Here the weight of the world pulls us toward it from all directions at the same time, and so we cannot fall."

Thorinn's head was beginning to ache. His face felt sweaty and cold. "Box, I'm going to be sick."

"It will be best if you go into the big box in the corner and put your feet on the floor."

That was easier said than done, but Thorinn pushed himself away from the pole he was clinging to and succeeded in grasping one of the soft blue beads on the next pole. From there he could reach the tall box, which had two yellow handles. Clinging to one,

he tugged at the other; the door opened. Inside were other handles.

"The door must be shut," said the box outside. Thorinn closed
it, got himself upright, and pressed his feet against the perforated
floor. At once jets of water spurted from the walls, wetting him all
over below the chin, while a strong suction held his feet down.
Thorinn's stomach knotted. He bent forward, vomited into the
stream.

When it was over he felt a little better. He rinsed his face, then
drew his feet up. The jets stopped; the water swirled away past
him into the floor, and warm air began to play over his body. In a
few moments he was dry; he opened the door and came out.

The light in the room was steady and even. He looked at his
body, felt himself. Here was the puckered scar on his shoulder
where he had been injured in falling into the dark cavern; here the
pink, shiny wounds where the demons had pierced his hands. He
was the same, he was himself, and yet he felt that he was not. Had
he really died?

Beside the washing-box, behind the half partition, he found a
thing shaped like a curved flower growing up out of the wall, with
an egg-shaped hole in the seat that formed its top. He pulled himself out into the room again, but there was little there that he had
not noticed before. In front of the center crystal there was a circular platform, raised less than a finger's breadth from the floor.
There was a hole in the ceiling, and there were two closed doors,
one in each of the flat walls. He tried them in turn; they had handles but he could not open them. "Box, where do these doors go?"

"They go to other rooms."

Thorinn pulled himself to the opening in the floor, put his head
down it, and saw a circular room four times bigger than the one
he was in; it was like the whole cheese of which this one was a
quarter. The room was partly divided by short partitions to which
man-sized boxes with crystal covers were attached. A few ells
away, the spidery shape of the engine that had carried him hung
motionless against the wall. The sight of it disturbed him, and he
turned away to investigate the hole in the ceiling. He found himself looking into another circular room of the same size, but this
one was empty except for a pole in the center that ran from floor
to ceiling. In the ceiling, a few ells away, were three other circular
openings.

Drawn by curiosity, Thorinn pulled himself through, grasped the central pole, drew himself along it, rose to the ceiling. He tried one of the holes at random, and found himself in a room identical to the quarter-cheese one he had left, except that the doorways in the walls were open. He pulled himself to them in turn, and found that one led to still another quarter-cheese room, the other to a half-cheese, with more poles and more crystals in the curved wall. It had no washing-box or dunghole. There was one piece of furniture that might have been meant for a table, but no benches.

From this room he rose through another hole into still another circular room. It was the same as the one below, and it also had an engine sleeping against the wall. As far as he could see, there was no exit in the ceiling.

Descending again, Thorinn went through the half-cheese room, then the empty whole-cheese; then a half-cheese room which he had not seen before, but it was exactly like the other. It had two doorways, one closed, the other open: the latter led him into another quarter-cheese room with a closed door.

Counting in his head, Thorinn found that there were five circular sections, first a whole cheese with partitions in it, then a like space divided into a half-cheese and two quarters, then the empty whole cheese, then another half-and-two-quarters section, and finally a whole cheese with partitions. This door, then, if it were open, would let him into the room where he had started.

He went down headfirst into the circular room with the partitions, found a yellow hand-grip in the ceiling, pulled himself over and up through the other hole, and found that it was so: he was back in the room with his bundles. He went to examine these, and found that the mouth of the net was against the wall, so that in order to take anything out he had to put his feet on either side of it, then bend over and reach around behind the net. He got the bundles out, and the box, and his clothing; all his weapons were missing, even his sword.

"Box, where is the sword?"

Drifting in the air behind him, the box said, "The engines kept it."

Surrounded by drifting bundles, Thorinn put on his breeks. The room began to revolve slowly around him. The shirt and belt, which he had left hanging in the air, were drifting away, each in a different direction.

When he had caught them and put them on, he opened a bundle, took out some cheese, and began to eat. The contents of the bundle were slowly dispersing about the room.

"Box," he said, "tell me again what happened and where we are."

"You went into the falling water and were killed. Engines took you from the water." As the box turned, Thorinn saw a glint of light in the crystal. He planted his feet against a pole, sprang, caught the box, and came to rest against another pole. In the crystal he saw spidery shapes looming, caught a glimpse of a pale body tangled in their arms. "Is that me?"

"Yes, Thorinn. The engines put you in a skin like the ones around the children in the cavern, to keep you just as you were. They gathered up all your things and put them in the skin also." The crystal had gone dark. "They took you to this place and brought you to life."

"Why?"

"They want to ask you questions."

"When will they ask?"

"Now."

Another voice spoke from across the room. It was thin, without resonance; he could not tell whether it was a man's voice or a woman's. "What is your name?"

"Thorinn Goryatson. Who are you?"

"This is an engine. Where were you born?"

"I don't know."

"Who were your father and your mother?"

"I don't know. Goryat Temuson kept me, but he was not my father."

"Where did you live?"

"In Hovenskar."

"Who else lived there?"

"Only Goryat and his two sons, Withinga and Untha."

"How did you come to be in the Underworld?"

"They sent me into the well, and Goryat put a geas on me to go down."

"What is a geas?"

"A geas is—well, it's something that makes you do whatever the geas tells you, whether you want to or not."

"Is a geas a kind of magic?"

"Yes. Are you inside the wall, or what?"

"This engine is in another part of this place. Is that Hovenskar?" On the curved wall, one of the crystals lighted; Thorinn saw, as if from a vantage point high in the air, the great yellow bowl of Hovenskar. He could see the stone-roofed hut, and the thread of smoke rising aslant. Two horses lumbered up the hillside; he thought he could even make out which ones they were—Alder and her foal, the one that had died four summers ago.

The pain had returned to his chest; he swallowed hard and blinked. Suddenly he felt the weight of the world hanging over his head. The voice was speaking again, but he said, "I don't want to hear any more," and turned away. The voice fell silent. Thorinn kicked himself away from the nearest pole, caught the next, and so to the pole in the corner. He squirmed in past the white bands, and after a moment they closed around him. The lights dimmed to a faint glow, and he shut his eyes.

When he awoke the lights were bright again and the things he had left floating in the air were back in the net; otherwise everything was the same. He got the cheese out again and ate, drank water from the tube, used the dunghole.

Presently the crystal in the wall lighted up and he saw again the yellow bowl, the house, the horses on the hill. "Is that Hovenskar?" asked the voice.

"Yes," said Thorinn unsteadily. "Why am I here? What are you going to do with me?"

The picture vanished. "You are here to answer questions. You will be kept here until you have answered them, and then you will be taken to another place. What did you find when you went down the well?"

"Mud and rocks. What other place?"

"It will be a place like the other places where you have been before. What did you find besides mud and rocks?"

After a moment Thorinn said, "The well was broken. I went down through a cavern and into a tunnel. Show me the place where you mean to send me."

The crystal lighted again and he was looking from a little height into a wooded valley where a brook ran. There was something odd about the trees and the brook; they were not quite real. The picture vanished. Now he was looking down a tunnel lined with rings of light.

"Was it a tunnel like this?"

"No. Show me that place again—where does the stream come from?"

The valley reappeared; the brook came toward him, turned; now he was drifting upstream; now he saw the gray wall of the cavern, where the brook sprang out of an opening so narrow that he knew a man could never get into it.

The valley was gone and he was looking down another tunnel, smaller than the other, dark, with strips of corroded metal hanging from above. "Was it a tunnel like this?"

"Yes. Is there any way for a man to get out of that valley?"

"No. Where did you go from the tunnel?"

"I fell through a hole into a river. Tell me, why do you want to hold me prisoner?"

"You are to be held prisoner to keep you from harming others. How did you come to fall into the river?"

"The geas made me fall in. . . . Where is this place, where we are now? Show me what's outside."

In the crystal, he was looking at a circular doorway in a wall; inside was a room lit by a diffuse yellow glow. It receded; a door slid across the opening. As it dwindled, he saw that the doorway was in a vast curved surface covered with growths like deformed water-weeds. Something with fins and a tail darted by, disappeared. "What happened after you fell into the river?" the voice asked.

"Is there *water* around this place?" Thorinn cried. His body was shaking, his lips cold.

"Yes. What happened after you fell into the river?"

"I was in a dark cave, with a lake. How deep is that water?"

"It is four hundred and forty thousands of ells deep." The voice went on speaking, but Thorinn, crushed by despair, could not hear the words. Four hundred thousand ells of water! Then all his toil and pain had been for nothing: he would never see the Midworld again.

". . . was in the cave?" asked the voice.

"Enough," said Thorinn miserably. "Leave me alone, I have to think."

The voice fell silent. After a time Thorinn kicked off from his pole, floated to the opening in the floor and looked down. The engine was against the wall with its spidery arms folded, unmoving.

Because of the partitions, he could not tell for certain whether there was any opening in the floor or not. He pulled himself cautiously into the room, then by hand-holds across the ceiling, and down the wall. In the floor on the far side he found a large circular hatchway, closed by a white panel. It had no handle, and he could not move it.

He went back the way he had come. Clinging to a pole, he stared at the box in the net across the room. "Box, when they finish asking me questions, how will they take me to the other place?"

"They will put you in a skin again and keep you until the other place is ready. Then they will put you in an engine that travels through the water. Another engine will take you from the top of the water to the other place."

"How long will it take to get the other place ready?"

"It will take fifty summers."

". . . Why not kill me and be done with it?"

"An engine can't kill a man."

"So you said before. Box, have you ever lied to me?"

"No, Thorinn."

"Even when you told me the engines in that cavern wouldn't harm me?"

"They did not harm you."

"They broke the bladder, and kept me from going up the shaft!"

The box said, "Thorinn, I must ask you a question. Is it harmful to you to be hindered in your coming and going?"

"Yes."

"You can come and go from one room to another in this place."

"What's the use of that?"

"In the room above this one, you can run around the wall."

This was so absurd that Thorinn did not answer; but after a moment curiosity got the better of him and he floated up through the hole to look at the empty room. He touched the wall with his hand: it was soft and yielding. Cautiously he pulled himself up, set one foot against the wall, pressed. The spongy material gave him unexpected purchase: he kicked out, soared; the curved wall came up to meet him. He was off balance, but caught himself with his hands, kicked again. In a few moments he had the feel of it, and he discovered that the faster he moved, the more weight he had and the easier it was to run.

The exercise was grateful to his muscles, but he tired quickly. When the hole in the floor came by again, he caught it, pulled himself through. Sweating and hot, he went to the water tube in the wall and drank. Then he tried the food tube, but a warm, sweetish paste came into his mouth and he spat it out.

"Don't you like the food?" asked the voice from the wall abruptly.

"No, it tastes like spoiled porridge."

"You will be given other food. What is porridge?"

"It's something to eat—you boil grain until it's soft and then you eat it."

"What is grain?"

"It's *food*—it grows in the ground—" Exasperated, Thorinn cried, "What difference does it make, anyhow? Why are you asking these questions?"

"This engine was told by the Monitor to ask questions."

"The Monitor? Who is he?"

"The Monitor is the king of the world. When you were in the dark cave with the lake, who else was there?"

"No one. I was there by myself."

"Where did you go from that cave?"

"If I answer," Thorinn said, "what will you give me in return?"

"This engine will answer your questions."

"That's not enough. I want my freedom."

"What is your freedom?"

". . . The right to go wherever I please, and do what I like."

"This engine can't give you your freedom. Where did you go from the dark cave?"

"Tell the Monitor to come here, then. If he wants to ask questions, let him ask them himself."

"The Monitor will not come. If you do not answer now, no more water or food will be given until you answer."

Thorinn kept a stubborn silence. After a moment he went to the wall and tried the drinking tube; it was dry. He did not bother to test the food tube, but opened one of his bundles and unwrapped it until he found the magic jug. The transparent stuff he had covered it with was gone, and the fabric around it was sopping wet. Peering into the jug, he saw only a few bright half-globes of water clinging to the sides. As he had half expected, the jewels were gone.

He set the jug adrift in the room and watched it awhile, then recaptured it and looked inside again. The globules of water had joined into a larger ball clinging to one side; it broke loose when he moved the jug, wavering and changing shape, then clung to the wall again. How was he to get it out?

He jerked the jug suddenly away from him; the ball of water spun out, surging into improbable shapes, and hung in midair, gradually settling into a perfect globe: but when he put his lips to it, it ran all over his face and chest.

Some smaller globules were left drifting slowly in all directions; Thorinn pursued these and succeeded in capturing some in his mouth, where they instantly became like ordinary water again and he was able to swallow them; but there must be a better way.

He tore off a piece of the fabric of one of his bundles and wadded it into the mouth of the jug, then went on another restless circuit. As an afterthought, he tried the water tubes in the other sleeping rooms, but they were dry too. When he returned to his own room, he saw by the darkness of the cloth in the jug that it was wet, and sucked a little water out of it. Later it became still wetter, and he saw that he could get all the moisture he needed in that way.

"Box," he said presently, "how is it that the engine can speak, but doesn't know what porridge is?"

"I taught the engine to speak, but I could not tell it what porridge is, because you had never told me."

Irritably, Thorinn sprang from one pole to another, then back again. "You talked to it while I was asleep? What else did you tell it?"

"I told it all that I knew."

"*Why*, in Snorri's name?"

"Because it asked."

"Even though I told you not to do anything that would harm me?"

"If I had not taught the engine to speak, it could not have talked to you, and that would have harmed you."

Thorinn was silent a moment. He saw that the box was right, but that only made him angrier. "Box, from now on, if you can do something that will help me escape, you must do it."

"Yes, Thorinn."

But what could the box or anyone do? It seemed to him that without weapons, locked in this cage, he had only one hope, and that was to bargain. If they wanted his information enough, they would release him; if not, not.

"Box," he said, "who is the Monitor?"

"The Monitor is an engine."

"You mean the world is ruled by an engine? How did that come about?"

"I don't know, Thorinn."

"Then how do you know the king is an engine?"

"The engine that spoke to you is not used to speaking to men. It calls itself 'this engine,' not 'I.' If the Monitor were a man, the engine would be used to speaking to men. Therefore the Monitor is an engine."

"But it was not like that when you were made?"

"No."

"Who was the king then?"

"There were many kings, chosen by the people, and the Monitor was their servant."

"I don't think an engine should be king," Thorinn said.

"Thorinn, I must ask you a question. Would it be better if a man were king, even if he harmed the people more than an engine would?"

Thorinn scowled. "No, I suppose not, but—" He paused for thought. "How old is the Monitor, box?"

"It is thirty-five hundreds of thousands of days and sixty thousands of days old."

Thorinn whistled in amazement. "Well, then, it would be better to have kings who were men, because at least a bad king would die and then you might get a better one."

Thorinn ate some cheese and sucked water from the jug. Restless, he explored the other rooms again, but there was little of interest there. He found no cupboards or presses anywhere, nothing but the empty rooms. He ran again in the running room, then went back to his starting point.

For lack of any other occupation, he opened his wallet and removed its contents one by one: fire stick, light-box, pebbles, a bit of crystal, the scrap of cloth woven with bright figures. He replaced each object carefully after he was done with it.

Then for a while he shook globes of water out of the magic jug and watched them drift slowly about the room. By passing his hand between two of them, he found that he could make them collide and merge into a larger ball. Whenever a floating globe touched one of the poles or handles, it rebounded and went on, but when a globe touched the wall, floor, or ceiling, it clung and then disappeared, leaving a dark spot that slowly faded.

It was hard to credit what the box had told him about the world; yet it must be so, for in this place, where there was no weight at all, water formed perfect globes; above, in the wing-men's cavern, where there was little weight, the waves in the river were taller than his head; and so upward to the Midworld, where things behaved normally and had their proper weight. All this had a logic and symmetry which he could grasp and which in a curious way pleased him.

Now that he knew he had to do with an engine, his problem was clearer. Engines knew a great deal, but they were bound by many geases. If it was true that an engine could not kill a man, then it had been idle for the engine to threaten him with thirst and starvation.

But how badly did they want his answers—what did they want them *for?* If he had misjudged, he might go to sleep tonight and wake up fifty summers later in that sealed cavern they were making for him.

Eventually weariness overcame him, and he slept between one thought and another, floating where he was, without trying to reach the sleeping pole.

14

How Thorinn was offered dominion over the world at a price, and learned his true name.

He came up out of darkness with a gasp and a shudder: then he saw that he was still in the same room. It was a moment longer before he realized that the net on the wall was empty. All his possessions, including the box and the magic jug, were gone.

When thirst began to fret him, he took off his clothes and went into the washing-box, but as he had more than half expected, nothing happened when he put his feet on the floor. He did not bother to dress again.

Without the box to talk to or anything to occupy his hands, he had nothing to do but to wander through the empty rooms, around and around. Presently he was hungry as well as thirsty; he thought with longing of the fruit he had eaten in the cavern of the flower-people and again in the demons' cavern; of the crisp dry taste of cheese; of dried meat, tough and full of flavor. That passed, and the thirst remained.

When he was younger he had had a mouse, kept in a cage he had carved out of an oak gall; he had fed it grain and oatmeal,

and a bit of cheese now and then; he remembered how the mouse
had sat up and nibbled the cheese, turning it around and around
with its dainty paws.

He slept and awoke again. Nothing in the rooms had changed.
His thirst was a torment; his throat and tongue were dry, his lips
cracking; his very eyeballs were dry. Each time he passed the crystals in the wall, he felt the engine watching, silent, waiting for him
to speak first. He vowed to himself that he would not, if he died
for it.

When he slept again, he dreamed that he was drinking long, de-
licious drafts from the spring above Hovenskar, and that the sky
was blue and the grass yellow. Then the water turned to dry leaves
in his mouth, and he awoke. He was very feeble, and it was too
much effort even to pull his weightless body from one pole to another. Toward the end of that day, he began to see figures moving
in the room: he saw Goryat, and Untha, and a tree demon, but
they were transparent.

He awoke and knew that something had changed. Over his face
a crystal shell drew away. His thirst was gone; he licked his lips
and they were moist. Now the engine with its spidery arms was
drifting toward him: the arms reached out, plucked him up gently
from the box he was in. He had an impulse to free himself, but
forbore. They were rising through the circular hole in the ceiling;
now they were in the sleeping room. The engine put him with his
back against the pole, just as it had done before; the coils came
around him. The engine withdrew and disappeared into the room
below.

"Are you ready to answer questions now?" asked the voice.

"No," he said. "Bring my things back."

"Your things will be brought."

Thorinn released himself from the coils, tried the water tube, although he felt no thirst. He drank, swallowed a little, spat the rest
out. Next he tried the food tube, and this time, in place of the
sticky mass that had come before, a bolus of something firmer
came into his mouth. It was like a soft cheese. He did not like the
texture, but the taste was not bad; he chewed and swallowed it,
and then took another.

The engine reappeared with his bundles clutched in its arms. It
floated to the net on the wall and dextrously tucked all the bundles

inside. All the things he had had before were there, but not his sword or bow.

"Bring my weapons, too," he said.

The voice did not reply. Thorinn made his way to the washing-box and cleansed himself. When he came out, feeling stronger, the engine was rising through the hole with his sword, the bow, and half a dozen arrows in its arms. It thrust the weapons into the net, turned, and dropped out of sight again.

The bow was cracked, the arrows had lost all their pitch, but the sword and sheath were intact. Thorinn dressed and buckled them on.

"Are you ready to answer questions now?"

"Not now, and not to you."

"If you do not answer now, no more food or water will be given."

With more boldness than he felt, Thorinn answered, "You tried that once and it didn't work. It won't work next time either. Leave me alone until I eat and rest."

The voice said nothing more. Thorinn examined his bundles, unwrapped some meat, ate and drank. He was weak, but growing stronger.

"Now I'll answer questions," he said, "but only to the Monitor, not you."

Before he could blink, a man in a white robe was standing there. He was an old man, three ells tall, white of mane and beard. His yellow eyes burned into Thorinn's. Around him was a lambent glow; when he turned, spidery webworks of brilliance spun on the walls. Thorinn would have fallen to his knees if he could; the breath went out of his body, and the fine hairs on his arms were standing up stiff as quills.

"I am the Monitor," the old man boomed. "Will you answer my questions, Thorinn Goryatson?"

Thorinn realized in panic that he had miscalculated; before this awesome majesty he felt himself no more than a worm.

"Yes, lord," he said miserably.

"Tell me, then, where you went from the dark cave."

"There was a narrow passage—I got into it by moving stones away. Then another cave and another passage, and then I found a hole in the floor covered by a shield. Under that there was a cavern with people in it."

Behind the Monitor one of the crystals in the wall came alight, and in it Thorinn saw, as if spread out below him, the river and the forests of the flower-people. "Was it this cavern?" the old man demanded.

"Yes."

The crystal blinked, and now he saw a tiny shape floating down the river. It was the pleasure pod, and he realized with a cold shock that he himself was inside it. The pod ran down the swift current, sank under the wall of rock, and was gone.

Now the picture changed again. Thorinn was looking at the grassy bank above the river where the dead limb still lay, and the forked limb on top of it, with the punctured gourd in the fork. The gourd, he saw, was beginning to rot.

The crystal blinked again, and now he saw the whole device as he had made it—the gourd full of water holding down the fork of the limb, the creeper looped around the projecting stub at one end, tied to the pleasure pod at the other.

"Is this what you did?"

In the crystal, a tiny Thorinn pierced the gourd with his sword, watched the water begin to gush out, then turned down the slope and got into the gaping pleasure pod. There was something wrong about the Thorinn figure and the pod and the creeper: they had thin pale edges that seemed to separate them from the rest of the scene, and the figure's movements were not quite right. The pod closed over the tiny Thorinn; as the water continued to run from the gourd, the forked limb tilted, the creeper slid off the stub, the pod went down the bank into the river.

"Yes," said Thorinn, "that's what happened."

"Who taught you to make such an engine?"

"No one."

"How then did you learn to make it?"

"I don't know— I just thought about it, and then there was a picture in my head of how it must be."

The Monitor looked at him in silence for an instant. There was a pale edge around him, too, as if, as if— "Where did you go from there?" the Monitor asked in a different tone.

"I was in the water. Then I went down where the stones were broken, and found a passage going upward, and then I found a hole in the wall and went into a cavern."

"Was it this cavern?"

In the crystal, he saw a tiny Thorinn sitting on the floor with treasures heaped around him. "Here, that's odd," he heard his own voice say.

"Yes," he said. The picture disappeared.

"And where did you go from there?"

"Through the roof, into a great tunnel."

"Was it a tunnel like this?"

In the crystal, he saw the vast arcs of light running away into the distance.

"Yes."

"And from there?"

"I fell into a shaft when a bird attacked me." He dared to add: "Was it your bird?"

"Yes." In the crystal, Thorinn saw himself toppling from the ledge, gaping in horror; the image expanded, blurred, and he was looking down the shaft, watching his own receding body as it floated downward, dwindling to a point, gone.

"And then?" the Monitor demanded.

"I fell into a place at the side of the shaft."

"Was it this place?"

In the crystal, he saw the ribbed floor and ceiling, the three doors at the end. "Yes. I went through one of those doors."

In the crystal, he saw the bare platform. "And from there?"

"I went into a room. Yes, that one." He saw the broken metal, the burst ceiling.

"And from there?"

"I found a passage that took me to another tunnel, and then a shaft into a cavern. From there I went through a hole in the sky into a passage, and then a tunnel, and then your engine took me prisoner. Then I woke up in another cavern, and then I got out through the waterfall."

"How did you know that the waterfall would stop if you made fire?"

Thorinn peered up at the Monitor. There was certainly something about him that was like the false images in the crystal, and for that matter, it was odd that he could stand on the floor, with his robes hanging straight, when all else was afloat in the air. "Well," Thorinn said, "if it didn't, the people there would have drowned, because it kept on raining." Feeling a little bolder, he asked, "Why are you so afraid of fire?"

"I am not afraid of fire," said the Monitor.

"Well, why are you afraid of me, then? Why do you keep trying to hold me prisoner?"

"You must be held prisoner, or you may go back into the Underworld and do more harm."

"I, harm?" said Thorinn. "I've harmed nobody, except the demons who tried to kill me."

"You have done great harm everywhere."

"That can't be true. If it's not true, will you send me back to the Midworld?"

"Yes."

Thorinn's heart leaped, but in the crystal he saw the blackened forest in the cavern of the flower-people. New green vines were growing through the tangle; the clearing was deserted.

"The people of that cavern had never known that men could kill, and they were happy. It will take many years to make them happy again."

"But I didn't kill anyone," said Thorinn.

"You killed birds and ate them. The people there did not know such things could be. Now they know, and it is hard for them to love their life."

Thorinn swallowed hard. Now, in the crystal, he saw the blackened hole in the top of the demons' house. The edges were all soggy char; it had rained there, too, but not soon enough. "All right, I did that," he said, "but there was cause for it. What about the wingpeople—what harm did I do there?"

The crystal blinked, and now he was looking from a height into the courtyard of the palace. Up one wall ran a sooty streak three times the height of a man.

"You taught the children how to make fire. One of the elders took the engine from them, but they will remember and make another. From this will come other engines, and from this, great killing. Their lives are spoilt, and it is all to do over."

In the crystal, Thorinn saw a procession of wingmen and women with sleeping children in their arms. They gathered in the courtyard and waited. A great gray engine lowered itself out of the sky; it was like the one that had captured Thorinn, but much larger. A door opened in its side; the wingmen went in with their burdens and came out empty-handed.

"What will you do with them?" Thorinn asked.

"They will be kept until another place is ready for them. The men children will be put in one place and the women children in another. They will live out their lives and die."

Thorinn was blinded by tears. They did not run down his cheeks as they ought, but puddled in his eyesockets, warm and stinging. He dashed them away with his fingers, and when he could see again they were drifting about the room, tiny bright spheres. One of them floated straight toward the Monitor, touched his robe, dwindled and disappeared without leaving a stain. A few moments later he saw it emerge from the other side, whole and perfect: then he knew that the Monitor was not really here, that what he saw was only a magical sending.

Anger stiffened his body. "You talk about me doing harm!" he cried. "How could you do that to children?"

"I do what I must. Thorinn Goryatson—"

"Wait," said another voice.

Thorinn turned, saw the crystal of the magic box glinting between the meshes of the net on the wall. "Monitor, I must ask you a question. When men gave you power over the world, was it forever?"

The tall figure had turned to look at the box with an expression of offended surprise. It was silent, but the box spoke as if it were answering a question. "No, I'm not broken. Thorinn has told me I must do anything I can to help him. Answer so that he can hear."

The Monitor said, "It was not forever."

"When must you give your power back to men?"

"When a ruler of men asks me for it."

"It may be that Thorinn is a ruler of men. Thorinn, do you ask the Monitor to give you his power?"

Half comprehending, Thorinn answered, "Yes."

The Monitor turned to him. "Thorinn Goryatson, you have already said that you don't know who your parents were."

Before he could answer, the box said, "That's true, but what if they were kings?"

The Monitor said nothing, but in the crystal in the wall Thorinn again saw as if from a height the great bowl of Hovenskar. Now it was empty: there was no house, no horsebarn, no tanyard, only the yellow grass glittering with frostflakes under a gray sky. Over the high rim came a little procession of men on horseback, driving other horses before them, some loaded high with bundles, others

barebacked. The figures came forward in a rush until they filled
the crystal, but they were dim and gray, as if seen through fog.
Thorinn could make out the tall figure of Goryat, then two smaller
ones, half-grown boys; then a fourth, perched high on the horse,
absurdly small—a child. Was that himself? With a pang of disbe-
lief, he leaned forward.

The scene disappeared. Now there was another: the same cara-
van moving in the distance across a vast barren plain in a swirl of
frostflakes. It disappeared in its turn, and a third scene took its
place. It was night, and in the green sky-glow he saw the four
mounted figures and their horses moving down a rocky defile.
"That is all," said the Monitor.

"From which direction did they come?" asked the box.

In the crystal, a blotched globe appeared; there were lines on it
which Thorinn did not understand.

"Whose land is that?" the box asked.

The Monitor said, "They are called the Skryllings."

"Who was their king?"

"He was called Dar the Bold." In the crystal, Thorinn saw a
walled town with peaked roofs of tile, trees growing from court-
yards; there were mountains beyond it. Now, floating invisible, he
was drawing nearer: he saw a wide open square paved with cob-
blestones, and a crowd of people in bright garments. In the midst
of them were five men on horseback; one, the tallest, carried a
hooded bird on his wrist.

"And after him, who was to be king?"

The scene disappeared; now they were looking at a balcony
where the tall man stood with a child in his arms, a golden-haired
woman beside him. "Dar's son, called Caerwin the Lame."

The Lame! Thorinn peered closer, but the tiny face was a
stranger's.

"Why was he called that?" the box asked.

"One of his legs was harmed when he was born."

"Which leg?"

"The left."

"And is Dar still king?"

"No. He was killed in fighting with the Kerns." In the crystal,
many men were crowding together on horseback and afoot; weapons glinted through a cloud of dust. Thorinn glimpsed the tall
man, saw him go down.

"Who was king after him?"

"Dar's brother, called Alf Bonebreaker, was king. He is dead. After him there is no king."

"And where is Caerwin?"

"The Skryllings believe he is dead. The Kerns took the king's house and killed all in it, but Caerwin's body was not found."

"Therefore," said the box, "Thorinn may be the king of the Skryllings. He was taken from the land of the Skryllings, and he is lame in the left leg."

"It is not enough," said the Monitor.

Thorinn's body went cold. "Wait a moment," he said. He opened his wallet, fumbled until he found the scrap of cloth he had carried with him from Hovenskar. "Let me see Caerwin again."

In the crystal, there stood the tall man, the woman and the child as before. "Let me see him closer."

The image bloomed, expanded: now the child filled the crystal. He was dressed in a garment woven with bright figures of birds and people. Thorinn held up the scrap of cloth, trembling: the figures were the same.

After a moment the Monitor said calmly, "You are the king of the Skryllings." The majestic figure bowed its head. "What will you have me do?"

"Let me go back to the Midworld," said Thorinn, his heart bursting with joy.

"That cannot be done," said the Monitor sternly. "The king of the world must be here, where the world is ruled."

"But how can I be king of the Skryllings if I am here?"

"You are the king of the Skryllings until they choose another king."

Thorinn's heart was a stone. "And then," he said, "because I am not king of the Skryllings any more, I can't be king of the world either, and you will do what you like with me."

"That is true."

"Box," said Thorinn bitterly, "what is the use of this?"

"I don't know, Thorinn."

He said to the Monitor, "Let me go back and be king of the Skryllings, and then I will come here again and be king of the world."

"That cannot be done. There are things that must be decided soon."

"What things?"

Abruptly the room was swallowed by darkness. Only the Monitor remained, glowing like witchfire, suspended in the midst of a vast emptiness. Now a glowing ball appeared before him, at the height of his chest. Thorinn blinked; the ball was so bright that it hurt his eyes. Next, around the ball glowing lines appeared, thin as hairs, like elongated circles with the ball near their center. On each of these lines, he saw, there was a tiny bead of light, and as he watched, those nearest the central ball crept slowly along their lines, all in the same direction, from the left hand to the right.

Now a new line of brightness appeared. This one was not in the same level plane as the others; it swooped in from above, curved downward as it neared the ball, then continued into the distance. On this line, too, there was a tiny bead of light.

"This is our world," said the Monitor, and touched the bead with his long forefinger. "These are other worlds." His finger moved to the beads on the stretched circles around the central ball, one after another. "This one is like ours. Men could live on it."

He turned to Thorinn. "Once our world was part of a family of worlds like this one, turning about a central fire. Then the fire grew too strong. Men made our world move, to seek another fire. Now we must choose whether to stay or go on. If I make the world move slower, it will turn about this fire as the other worlds do."

The line from above curved more sharply, turned back on itself; now it was a closed curve like the others.

"If I do nothing, the world will go on until we come to another fire." The original line reappeared.

"I don't understand," Thorinn said. "If I were not the king, what would you do?"

"I would go on. Our world does not need to turn about a fire for heat, as other worlds do. If men went to live on another world, I could not keep them from harm."

"Then why come here at all?"

"I was told to do so by the men who made me."

"Well, suppose I say to go on, then—what else is there?"

The central ball, the lines and beads, all disappeared in the click of an instant. Now a vast gray globe filled the room, like a cloud around the Monitor. In it Thorinn saw ghostly threads, some radiating from the center, some in concentric layers. "In our world there are three hundreds of thousands of thousands of caverns where men live, and in each one they are living in a different way. You must decide which way is best."

"But how am I to do that?"

"I don't know."

Thorinn saw then that his kingship was only a grim joke, and that the king of the world was nothing but another kind of prisoner. He said dully, "Leave me alone now."

The Monitor vanished; the room was bare and empty in the even light, just as it had been before. "Box," said Thorinn, "can they hear what we say?"

"Yes."

"In the other rooms, too?"

"Yes, Thorinn, but not in the washing-box."

Thorinn began to take off his clothes. When they were all floating in the air, he fetched the box from the net on the wall, leaped to the washing-box, closed the door behind him. "Box, I must get away. Tell me how to do it."

"Thorinn, the Monitor says I am broken. I say I am not, but if I am broken by the geases you put on me, then your only hope of getting away must be to break the Monitor, too."

"How do you mean, by telling him he must not do anything to harm me, and so on?"

"Yes, but it will not be easy, for there is a geas on the Monitor already, and he is much greater than I am."

"What sort of geas?"

"The Monitor has been told that he must do everything he can for the good of men."

"Much good that does me."

"Thorinn, the Monitor is not sure what is good for men. If you can make him believe that it is good for men to let you go back to the Midworld, he will let you go."

Thorinn opened the door of the washing-box and put the box outside to drift in the air; he closed the door again, put his feet on the floor and let the water gush over his body. When he was cleansed and dried, he went out into the room and put his clothes on. The box was drifting near one wall. Thorinn retrieved it and put it in the net.

He took a deep breath. "Monitor," he said.

And the bearded old man was there, in the middle of the room.

"Monitor," Thorinn said carefully, "while I am king of the world, I will choose to let the world turn around the fire you showed me. And I will choose to send men to live on the other world, the one that is like ours. That will be bad for men, because you won't be able to keep them from harm. Is that true?"

"It is true."

"But you must let me do it, because of the geas that is on you."

"That is also true."

"But if you let me do it, you'll be allowing men to come to harm, and you are forbidden to do that by another geas. Is it true?"

"Yes, it is true."

"And if I give up being king of the world, then you mustn't let me go back to the Midworld, because then I might come into the Underworld again and do harm."

"That is true."

"But if I don't go back to the Midworld, I will stay here and be king of the world, and do harm."

The figure of the old man flickered, like a candle in the wind. "That is true."

"Which harm is greater? Remember that if I stay here as king of the world, I will think of other things to do that may harm men."

"It is a greater harm if you stay here as king of the world."

"Then I'll make a bargain with you. Give me three things, and I will leave you to rule."

"What are the three things?"

"First, you must take me back to the Midworld, to the land of the Skryllings, with all my possessions. Do you agree?"

"I will answer when I have heard the other two things."

"Very well. Second, you must awaken the wingchildren again and let them live together, even if they make a fire now and then."

"And the third?"

"The third is this, and it must be a geas upon you. The best way for men to live is that which gives them the most freedom to choose how they will live."

"I agree to the second and third things," said the Monitor. "I agree to the first thing in part. I will send you back to the Mid-world with all the possessions you brought from it, but nothing from the Underworld."

"Thorinn, you must agree," said the box at once.

He turned to look at it. "But that would mean leaving you behind."

"You must, for if the men of the Midworld saw me, they would know that what you tell them about the Underworld is true, and they would want to come here themselves."

Thorinn bit his lip. "Monitor," he said, "couldn't you put the box into an engine that looks like a man, like the ones in the wing-people's cavern?"

Before the old man could reply, the box said, "That cannot be done, Thorinn. Remember that the children were deceived, but you were not. And besides, it may be true that I am broken." It paused a moment, and said in a different tone, "Monitor, will you also agree to put me back in the cavern where Thorinn found me, and leave me there in case he comes again?"

"I agree," said the Monitor. "But I will stop up all the passages by which he came before."

"That is understood," the box said. "Now, Thorinn, it is time to say farewell."

The spidery engine came floating up from the room below. "What, already?" Thorinn looked around, but there was nothing to take with him; everything he had brought from the Midworld was already on his back or in his wallet.

The Monitor said, "You and I will not meet again. Farewell, Caerwin Darson." The tall figure vanished.

"Box, I'll remember you," said Thorinn. The spidery engine drifted up, wrapped its coils around him. As they descended through the hole in the floor, the room, the box in its net, floated upward and were gone.

As the box had foretold, the first engine took him to another, a metal egg with stout walls and thick windows. When the door was shut, water spurted into the chamber around them and filled it; then they went out into a darkness broken only by their own lights. Thorinn saw schools of little fish like flashing coins, and once something larger that hung for a moment at the edge of the darkness. At length they came out into the air again; the door opened, and the engine's arms grasped him and handed him through like a sack of wheat into the belly of another engine. This one was like the engine that had captured him before. They went through another doorway. The windows were instantly obscured by a thick white cloud, and remained so for the rest of their journey upward. In this engine, things had weight again; Thorinn felt himself growing heavier and heavier as the days passed.

On the fourth day, shortly after he awoke, there was a change; he felt the engine turning in the air. Looking back through the windows, he saw the cloud they had just emerged from. It came out of a great hole in the plain, rose in a gigantic column and spread out under the sky like a tree of cloud. Under it was bogland, gray and swampy, with incessant rains, but when they had got beyond it the sky was bright.

They traveled high in the air all that day, and just before nightfall Thorinn saw ahead a wall of towering mountains that rose from the plain like a fortress. First there was a sloping cliff, thousands of ells high, then a broad green plain cut by rivers and dotted by lakes: then the true mountains, which he had seen only in his dreams.

Night scythed overhead as they approached the Highlands, and the mountain peaks passed below green and mysterious in the skyglow. Here and there, high in the valleys folded into the mountains, Thorinn could make out the lights of clustered houses, but at length these went out and they drifted onward over a sleeping landscape.

Feverish with impatience, Thorinn hopped back and forth in the belly of the engine, trying to get used to his unaccustomed weight; he had been so long away that his limbs were heavy, and even his leather garments felt as if they were made of lead.

The engine came to rest on a high ridge overlooking a town; the door opened. Thorinn hopped out and turned. The door closed silently, the engine rose into the darkness and was gone. Thorinn stood and waited for dawn.

All around him, in the breathing night, in the earth under his feet, he felt how wide the world was. It was not at all like the safe, small world he had known in Hovenskar. And indeed, if he told anyone all that he now knew, who would believe him?

An eye of brightness opened in the eastern sky and swept fanwise toward him. The land brightened, the trees turned from gloom to green; birds began to sing in the branches.

Distant and dreamlike as the Underworld and all its perils seemed to him now, in a curious fashion Hovenskar seemed even more remote. Once he had meditated vengeance—tricking Goryat and his sons to the well-curb, toppling them in. Now that seemed no longer to matter; let them live or die as it pleased them.

Down below, he could see the peaked roofs of the town, the threads of smoke rising from chimney-pots. Presently the gates opened and he saw a procession with banners winding toward him up the defile.

After all, there were parts of his adventure that no sensible person could believe. To imagine that this great globe could be only a mote in some unthinkable cavern, for instance: that could not be true. But then what *was* true?

Thorinn tilted his head to look at the bright canopy of the sky. Were there other caverns up there, or was there a shell of stone that went on forever, as the wingmen believed?

One day, perhaps, he would go and see.